ALL
WOULD
── BE ──
HEROES

JIM MAHER

ALL
WOULD
— BE —
HEROES

TATE PUBLISHING
AND ENTERPRISES, LLC

Published by Tate Publishing & Enterprises, LLC
127 E. Trade Center Terrace | Mustang, Oklahoma 73064 USA
1.888.361.9473 | www.tatepublishing.com

Tate Publishing is committed to excellence in the publishing industry. The company reflects the philosophy established by the founders, based on Psalm 68:11,
"The Lord gave the word and great was the company of those who published it."

Book design copyright © 2016 by Tate Publishing, LLC. All rights reserved.
Cover design by Albert Ceasar Compay
Interior design by Shieldon Alcasid

Published in the United States of America

ISBN: 978-1-68333-742-3
1. Fiction / General
2. Fiction / War & Military
16.04.20

I am dedicating my story to America's Vietnam Veterans, especially the dozens that I have met over the last forty-six years. Their memories of service and how they tried to recover after coming back to their homes in America is what inspired me to write this book and tell the stories that it contains.

I would like to thank each and every Vietnam Veteran who has served our country.

Acknowledgments

THE STORY THAT is being told was written from my soul. I have my great friend and fellow author Christine J. Gilbert, who helped to give life to my story by taking the time to make additions and corrections that gave it life. Her input has been inspiring and humbling. She understood how important this work was because she is also a Veteran. Thank you from the bottom of my heart.

Contents

Preface

THERE ARE THOUSANDS of stories to be told about the heroics of American military personnel during the Vietnam War. Many have been published, but so many others remain hidden within the minds of the Vietnam veterans, hidden so deeply and painfully, they do not want to recount or even remember them.

I was not a military warrior. I was not exposed to enemy fire of any kind and didn't suffer wounds from our enemies during my time in Da Nang, South Vietnam, in 1970. I was only in country for less than three months on temporary assignment and seldom ever left our base except to make deliveries to other facilities in the Da Nang region. But I have heard many private stories from the men who were in the worst of the battles, usually when we had both had too much to drink. I have also read and heard about other Sailors, Marines, Airmen, and Army soldiers, and their experiences in a thankless bloody war that separated our nation.

The characters and the events in these stories are fictional, but they are based on events that either did happen because I was told about them, or they very likely happened based on the stories told in the bars, clubs, and other gathering points for veterans. The stories are constructions of my imagination based on what did and what could have taken place.

This is a work of respect, love, and passion for our Veterans then and now. If you are not a Veteran but do care about them and what they have been through, this book will keep your attention, and you will better understand and appreciate their sacrifices, their bravery, and their patriotism. No one could ask more from a Soldier, Sailor, Marine, or Airman than what they demanded of themselves. Please respect their service and thank them whenever you have the opportunity.

1

Facing Fear

Tom

THERE WAS SOMETHING wrong, but he couldn't define it. It was a feeling he had not experienced before, a feeling that he was in danger, a feeling of dread and fear, yet he knew he had to persevere.

He had made it this far, had survived longer than he had hoped, yet he feared this may be his moment. His time may have finally come. But he knew he couldn't turn back. He could not allow his fellow soldiers to be tortured and humiliated at the hands of the enemy. If this was his time, so be it; he must do the right thing.

Tom lay as flat as he could on the jungle floor. Surrounded by vegetation and insects of every kind, Tom plotted his moves and pictured his actions within himself. He had never attempted or even been trained to do this, but again, he wasn't turning back. He watched the Viet Cong soldiers' activities and began to pick up on their routine. Over the course of several hours, he began to see a pattern developing, one that had moments, sometimes several minutes, where the guards were preoccupied or away from their riverside encampment. He continually counted the enemy soldiers and tracked the moments when they were at their lowest numbers, sometimes as few as two but other times as many as six.

It was critical for him to pick the right time to attack, assuming that one man could launch an attack, so he was confronting the least number of enemy soldiers, increasing his chances of success and even survival.

The overcast skies that provided only the dullest of sunlight began to grow even darker as the sun began its descent. He debated whether it was better to jump them during the day or wait until nightfall when his vision would be even more limited. As he continued to evaluate the situation, his answer was provided as the evening quickly turned into night, although he did allow a procrastinating voice in his head to try to convince him to wait until the next morning. His hope was that there would be a smaller number of guards during the night hours so his chances would be improved.

All six of the Viet Cong soldiers gathered at their makeshift fire and cooked their rice and whatever else they would eat. The putrid smell of meat or fish or whatever it

was almost made him puke. He committed at that point
to not attempt to eat any of their leftovers, not even the
rice. He wondered how in the world they could eat that
crap! The four American soldiers were offered some what
looked like watered-down rice, but they were too weak to
even eat. When the American soldiers refused to eat, they
were kicked, slugged, and cursed. The six enemies laughed
at their suffering and the hurt they had put on these near-
death men. Tom's resolution to free them and kill the enemy
soldiers became even stronger, not only because of the
humiliating treatment of the Americans but because this
was war, and people had to fight and kill the enemy, or they
would be killed. He knew that he was doing the right thing
and would act when it was the best opportunity to free the
Americans and kill the enemy who stood in his way. He
hoped that he would find the courage and overcome his
fears to do this.

He was correct in his assumption that there would be
fewer guards during the night, as four of the guards boarded
their boat and motored away back to the river and upstream.
The two remaining guards checked the Americans to make
sure they were secured for the night, not appearing to
care whether they were still alive. One guard prepared his
bedding, and the other began his guard of the perimeter,
which was only about ten feet around the campfire.

Tom waited at least an hour to make sure none of the
other Viet Cong returned and figured the one guard would

be sleeping and the other relaxed and not expecting anything beyond the normal jungle noises and animal movements. Tom took a deep breath, said what he remembered of the prayers he learned in his youth, and began to execute his plan.

2

The Greetings Letter

Tom was a high school survivor. He wasn't a bad student, not a great student, just middle of the class. He wasn't athletic, although he tried playing football his freshman year. He'd ridden the bench and decided it wasn't worth the work. In fact, a lot of things in high school ended up not being worth the work. He was definitely interested in girls, but they weren't very interested in him, except as a friend; we all know what that means. He wasn't into band or choir, drama, or any other extracurricular activity. Tom tried smoking cigarettes, and to him they tasted awful; he tried drinking beer, which he liked, but it made him feel weird after only one or two, so he didn't drink beer that often.

For Tom, life was okay, nothing exciting. He was just getting by. He had a few acquaintances, but his best friend was really his younger brother, Jack. Jack looked up to him because Tom was two years older. They didn't do much, just drove around in their mom's car when she let Tom drive.

Tom didn't pay much attention to the news or what was going on in the world. As you can probably determine, Tom was just kind of going through his teen years with nothing getting too much of his attention.

As high school graduation approached, his dad asked him, "What do you plan to do after high school?" He hadn't expected the question, so he answered honestly with, "I don't know."

Tom's dad did not like his answer. He said, "You need to figure it out because it is time for you to stand on your own two feet."

Tom thought, *Why? Life is good. Why change it?* But he knew that's not what they wanted to hear, so he said, "I will think about it and maybe talk to the guidance counselor at school." Of course, he would have to find out who that was.

After he went to the Administration office at his high school and found out who the guidance counselor was, Tom made an appointment with her and arrived at her office almost on time.

The counselor reviewed his academic records, aptitude tests, and whatever other limited information his record contained. She told him that in her opinion, college was a long shot, although junior college (juco) might be a good way to find out if it was meant for him. Another option was a trade school, like studying to be a welder or an electrician. Since Tom wasn't very good with his hands, he didn't think that would be a good idea. He decided to give junior college a try since it was only thirty miles from home. Maybe his parents would buy him a car so he could drive back and forth. The counselor gave him the information about the college, which he filled out and returned it to her the next week. Because he was graduating from a high school in the juco's region, he would automatically be accepted. He thought, *This continuing education thing might be all right!*

He went home and told his parents he had decided to go to the junior college; they were shocked but supportive until he asked for a car. His father said, "We will help you buy a car, but you will have to get a job to pay your half and to pay the insurance and keep it gassed up and serviced. A vehicle is a big responsibility, and you have to be very serious about taking care of it."

Tom really wanted a car, so he assured his dad that he would take it very seriously and would take good care of a car. He also agreed that he would find a job to do his part in paying for it. They agreed that as soon as Tom went to work, they would shop for a vehicle. Since Tom turned eighteen earlier in the year, he was able to find a job at a local manufacturing plant. He hated it from day 1, but knew he had to stick with it to get a car. When he received his first check, his dad took him car shopping, and they purchased a ten-year-old Ford.

The car was Tom's pride and joy, and he now felt like he had a reason to live, to be interested in life. He wasn't sure if he liked the responsibility, but he hoped he'd get used to it.

Tom worked full time all summer, being faithful about paying for the Ford and keeping it serviced and gassed. He and his brother cleaned it inside and out every Saturday, and they would drive it around town, showing it off. Life was good, and responsibility wasn't so bad after all. Then it was time to start college. He was able to go to part time at the factory so he could keep money coming in. He was enrolled in the basic required classes, a total of twelve semester hours.

Tom got off to a decent start, attending every day, even doing some studying on the weekends. He made it through his first semester with a solid C+ average. Second semester, he decided to take a couple of classes that might be more interesting. He enrolled in zoology and psychology. It was not a good decision.

He dropped zoology after two weeks, recognizing he wasn't going to pass, plus there was no way he wanted to work that hard. Even though it was Psych I, he was confused by how he could even hope to figure all this stuff out in his head, let alone try to explain it. He hung with it for the first half of the semester, but because he was failing, he withdrew so he didn't have to go to the class that he was not going to pass. He was now only attending six semester hours, so he started working more hours at the factory.

As the end of the semester approached, he wasn't sure if he wanted to keep going to college. The first part of May, he received a letter that would solve that issue.

The "Greetings" letter from the Selective Service was a complete shock. He had heard about the draft and had registered for it when he turned eighteen, but because he was in college, he didn't think he had to worry about it. He took the letter to his college advisor and was told that since he dropped the classes, he wasn't officially a full-time student, so he was no longer eligible for the student deferment. Since he had received the draft letter, it was really too late for the college to do anything. The advisor suggested he go to the armed forces recruiting offices and see if he could join instead of being drafted. That's what Tom did, but none of the services could get him enlisted before he was to report for his draft physical, except the Marines. He didn't think he was meant to be a Marine, so decided to just go ahead with the draft notice and report as required. He reported and passed the induction requirements. Tom was accepted into the US Army and shipped to basic training at Fort Leonard Wood, Missouri.

Immediately, Tom knew that he was not going to like the Army. He had never been into physical activity, let alone physical fitness, so he hated the marching and exercising and all the other physical activities they had to endure. There were probably other guys in worse shape than him, but he was definitely giving the worst effort of anyone in his company. In fact, his squad leader called Tom the worst soldier he'd ever seen, the worst in the Army! That did get through to him, and he did put more effort into the remainder of basic, although he still wasn't the soldier most of the rest of his company became. He had also not done well on the firing range or in the other combat exercises. But he finished and graduated with the rest of his company. Because he had done fairly well on his test scores, he was assigned to Postal Clerk Advanced Individual Training (AIT).

How great is this, he thought. *I'll be working in a post office while these other guys are out slopping through the swamps and jungles!* Needless to say, his smug looks did not endear him to his company. But they all went off to the AITs and would likely never see Tom again.

Tom did surprisingly well at Postal AIT. He liked the work. It was not too strenuous or too mentally taxing. He actually was going to finish toward the top of his class. It was quite a surprise, even to himself.

Orders came out two weeks before graduation, and when Tom opened his, he couldn't believe it. He was being assigned to the post office that was attached to the Army's I corps command near Da Nang, South Vietnam.

How is that possible? I'm one of the best in my class. I should be getting a stateside or European assignment.

Then someone reminded him that he and some of the others were draftees, so they were going to get the crappy assignments while the people who enlisted would get the better assignments. It didn't seem fair, but it's the way it was. Tom resigned himself to going to Vietnam, hoping he would be able to just stay on the base and do his job.

Tom went home from his training school and told his parents the news. His mother and dad were deeply traumatized. His mother said, "We watch the television news, and it's never good. All they talk about are all the American military people being killed or wounded, many losing their legs or arms or both and others being maimed for life. They also say American soldiers are being accused of atrocities and killing innocent women and children. I am heartbroken that you becoming a part of this and potentially suffering the same fate that so many other young Americans are enduring."

Even Tom's father became very emotional. Tom tried to assure them that he would be safe because he was a postal clerk and would not be in the jungles fighting the enemy or getting shot at constantly. Even as he tried to comfort them, he was privately very worried and afraid of what could happen.

When it was time for Tom to leave for Vietnam, there were very emotional good-byes with his family. But he bid his good-byes to his parents and brother, Jack, and boarded the train to take him to the airport for his flight to San Francisco and his two-week combat training school on the West Coast prior to going to his duty station near Da Nang, Vietnam.

Because of his improved behavior at the end of his basic training and during his postal clerk training school, he was an all-right student in combat training. His actions were good, but he didn't hesitate to complain about the daily rigors of the school and the harshness of the instructors. He didn't understand why a postal clerk should have to learn all this combat stuff when he would only be working in the post's mail office. His classmates grew tired of him and ignored him, leaving him isolated. He struggled because the others did not want to team with him even though he was performing all duties well. They just couldn't stand his complaining all the time.

At the end of the training, his frustrated training sergeant pulled him aside and angrily said, "Soldier, you had better get control of your mouth because if you don't, you will have serious trouble with your fellow soldiers. In Vietnam, everyone depends on each other, and all the units are teams. If you aren't accepted by your team, then you will be at great risk of not surviving."

Tom listened but didn't think his complaining was that bad and said that he would be better when he got to his duty station. The sergeant shook his head and walked away, knowing the problems that Tom was going to have if he didn't change his attitude.

All of Tom's classmates from survival school were transported directly to Travis Air Force Base north of San Francisco to board their flights to Vietnam. Many of them were on his flight directly to Da Nang, but none of them bothered to talk to him. Tom spent his time sleeping and checking out the stewardesses on the commercial flight. He wondered how long it would be before he saw an attractive American woman again. His thoughts turned to home and all that he was missing; he began to silently weep and feel very sorry for himself.

The flight was long, but the plane landed much sooner than Tom and most of the other soldiers had wished. As their plane pulled to a stop on the tarmac and they began to file off, Tom looked around the inside of the plane and took a deep breath, smelling America for the last time.

3

In-Country

As the troops assembled on the tarmac, unit representatives were calling out names one at a time. Tom heard his name and saw a smallish spec 4 looking his way. Tom walked to the specialist and handed him his orders. The specialist introduced himself as Mike Peters and said that he would be taking Tom on his introductory tour of the base, his barracks, the chow hall, the PX, and his duty station. He also took him to the bank to exchange his American money for Vietnamese money, piasters, because American money was the favorite black-market item for the Viet Cong. Tom met his Commanding Officer and his Postal Officer, as well as the First Sergeant of the unit and other members of the team. Specialist Peters showed him the duty roster and where Tom would be assigned. Because he was the newbie, Tom would be reporting at 0500 (5:00 a.m.) to start distributing mail that had arrived the night before. All the mail had to in the boxes by 0800 when the post office opened, so the early shift had to hustle to meet that requirement. Tom wasn't worried about that because he was confident of his ability based on his performance in postal school.

After being in country a few days and learning his way around and the basics of his job, he found out that this post office also serviced two other Army units nearby, including a Special Forces Group, and part of his duties would be to deliver mail to those units and make sure the Post's mail was properly distributed and their outbound mail was picked up and forwarded as quickly as possible. This would mean driving through roads surrounded by jungle and who knows what hiding in it. His fear level increased to a very significant level. To make it even worse, his fellow clerks showed him the duty roster. He asked what that was and was told that admin people rotated out on patrols with the regular soldiers. They usually stayed with the officer leading the patrol and were considered defensive, not actively engaging the enemy unless they had to. Now he knew this was bad. His worst fears were being realized. Being shot at, stepping on a mine, being hit by shrapnel and frags, shooting at another human being, the blood and cries of pain—it was very overwhelming to this slacker from the Midwest. He vowed to keep low, stay back away from the fights as much as possible, not do anything to put himself at risk, and get the hell out when he could.

As much as he hated it, Tom settled in to a routine of work and hanging out at the club. He hadn't been much of a drinker before, but it seemed to ease the stress of being continuously fearful. As his first patrol assignment approached, he experienced diarrhea, headaches, and cramps. His hands were shaky, and his knees wobbly as he climbed onto the Huey with the Ranger patrol. His fellow soldiers reassured him that this was a routine patrol and that encountering the enemy was unlikely. The confidence of the soldiers didn't help; Tom still complained about being with them, the bumpy flight, the crowded conditions, and the smelly bodies surrounding him. The soldiers ignored him and quit trying to reassure him. As the Huey landed, the squad jumped out and began spreading out in the brush. Tom disembarked as the copter came closest to the ground because he didn't want to risk spraining his ankle or falling down. He stayed close to the Lieutenant (LT) and the radioman and tried not to appear cowardly.

The patrol advanced to its objective, policed the area for signs of enemy activity, and, finding none, reported back to the LT that there were no signs of activity. The LT had the radioman call in the Huey. They reloaded and returned to their base. They had been out a total of five hours and did not encounter any enemy or signs of enemy activity.

Tom thought, *If they are all like this, no problem.* He didn't say anything positive out loud, just continued to complain about what he did and questioned why he had to be part of the patrol activities.

Patrol became part of Tom's routine, just like the rest of his duties. Traveling to the remote camps was sometimes more challenging than the patrols, but he managed to keep his head down and stayed safe. His patrols often did exchange fire with the enemy, but as always, Tom stayed away from the action as much as he could. Even though he was being protected by the members of his patrol, he still complained about everything, never once thinking it could be important to thank and praise them. He didn't just complain to his patrol members but also to the other postal clerks, his sergeant, and even the soldiers coming to the window at the postal hut.

As time continued and Tom's whining grew worse, people began to avoid him, going out of their way to keep from being around him, not willing to hear his tirades of discontent. He had always been a loner, but now he became even more isolated. He couldn't seem to stop the negative attitude. His sergeant and commanding officer both counseled him and warned him that his bad attitude could infect the troops, so he needed to stop being so negative. They even had the chaplain talk to Tom, but that didn't seem to work either.

As much as time seemed to drag on, Tom realized that he had reached the halfway point in his Vietnam assignment. He was due to go home in another six months, and he was also eligible for R & R, two weeks out of this godforsaken hell.

He selected Thailand and went to Bangkok for two fantastic weeks! Many other soldiers and sailors selected Bangkok because they people were very happy to see them, especially their money. Tom didn't care about the other Americans. He wanted to get away from the war and completely forget, at least for a while. He toured some of the most beautiful buildings he had ever seen, was fascinated by the way the Thai people dressed, and couldn't believe how attractive the women were. Beer and drinks were cheap in the bars and clubs, and it was amazing how many Thais spoke good English. The women were very friendly, and he was swayed into spending some of his money on their drinks and other favors. He was in heaven, at least for a few days. He couldn't remember the last time he smiled as much as he did for those two weeks.

Unfortunately, he had to board the plane back to Da Nang. Now his attitude was temporarily great, but within a few weeks, it sank back into the sewer. His complaints were worse as he found reasons to hate his returning from his R & R. Tom's brothers in arms didn't just ignore him. Now they pushed back, yelling at him to shut up, smacking him across the head and threatening to kick his ass if he didn't quit. He only tempered his complaining for brief periods of time before returning to the whining.

4

Left Behind

AFTER SEVERAL WEEKS of Tom's continuous whining and complaining, his turn came to go out on another patrol. Everything seemed to be routine as usual, with no enemy sightings or encounters. A couple of the Rangers told Tom that they needed his help in a remote area away from the landing zone (LZ).

Trying to avoid another beating, Tom reluctantly complied and thought, *This is a waste of my time!*

As they got farther from the LZ, the jungle became thicker and more difficult to walk through. They were at least five hundred yards away from the LZ, and there were no other troops visible, or even within hearing distance. The soldiers could hear the rotors of the Hueys returning for them.

Tom asked the Rangers, "Why did you bring me out here? What do you need me for?"

One of the soldiers replied, "We need you to assist us in bringing something back, but it isn't in sight yet."

They moved further into the jungle, and Tom thought, *Why is this so important?* As Tom heard the chopper, he began to think they would be turning back to the LZ soon. Suddenly he felt a severe pain to his head. Everything went black, and he was totally unconscious.

The two soldiers returned to the LZ and jumped on the Huey. The LT asked, "Where is Tom?"

One of the soldiers replied, "He must be on the other Huey, probably got mixed up again."

"Good enough," the LT said, accepting their logical explanation. "Let's get out of here!"

No one noticed that Tom hadn't returned until the next morning when he didn't show up for duty at the post office. The clerks actually enjoyed the peace and quiet until chow time, but they finally told the Sergeant and CO. The CO went to the patrol's LT, and the LT told him about the confusion about which copter Tom was on. He hadn't realized he wasn't back.

The two officers went to the post commander and reported that Tom was missing and how they believed it happened. They requested that a patrol be sent back to where the patrol had been the previous day to hopefully find Tom. The commander checked the latest communications and found that the area they were talking about had been occupied by the Viet Cong as they moved from village to village.

That activity made it unfavorable and unsafe for a small patrol. Based on the intelligence, they would have to strategize a much bigger operation to attempt the rescue. The enemy activity obviously made Tom's rescue very risky, and his safety was in doubt.

The black began to lighten to gray, and his head was throbbing as his eyes began to slowly reopen. Tom tried to get his bearings even with his head still very groggy. It was growing dark, and the skies were becoming cloudy and threatening. He rose to his feet and felt his head to check for blood or a lump as the reality of what had happened clarified. Tom had been intentionally left behind by the Rangers after one of them had knocked him unconscious with the butt of his M-16. He looked around where he had been dropped and saw his M-16 with two extra clips, obviously left by the two Rangers who had abandoned him. He was still wearing his pack, so he had some rations and water, along with a clean pair of socks and other basics.

The jungle was thick, and his view was limited, but he had to figure out the direction he needed to take. Tom tried to recall what he had learned in survival school, but because he hated it and complained about being there, he wasn't able to recall too many things that could have helped him now.

He did believe his best hope for finding his way back was to find a river or stream and follow its flow. The water would be flowing in a southern or eastern direction, and that was where the American outposts would be found. He tried to recall the terrain they had flown over to get to today's LZ and where the river or other body of water would be from his current location. Because he hadn't really paid attention due to complaining about being on patrol, he had no memory of any bodies of water. He recalled that the jungle and other foliage would become thicker going toward the water, so he thought his best bet was to keep pushing through the jungle to find water. Even though his head was still throbbing, he loaded on his pack and weapon and began struggling through the thick vegetation.

As he began his trek, he heard the sounds of vehicles behind him. He went back toward the LZ and glanced through the vegetation. He saw that the area was crawling with Viet Cong troops and trucks heading down a very narrow path. He quickly turned and pushed through the brush. The fear of capture or being spotted and shot was more than enough motivation that he needed to redouble his travel speed. After traveling at least half a mile, he stopped and listened for anyone possibly following him or any vehicle sounds that were growing closer. Hearing nothing but jungle noises, he allowed himself to rest briefly and to try and collect his thoughts. He was shaking uncontrollably and thought, *I'm not going to get out of the jungle alive or find my way out of here before I starve to death or get shot.* He had no confidence in his ability to find his way to a river or stream, let alone back to an Allied outpost or base. He had weapons that he wasn't very good with, food that he didn't like, and other equipment that he didn't even know how to use. He viewed his situation as hopeless, but he knew that he had to press on because he didn't want to die in the jungle.

As the skies grew darker, Tom thought he could hear the sound of running water. He pressed onward through the thickened scrub, and the sound of the water became more distinct. He knew this meant he was getting closer to the water. He reached the bank of a stream that looked to be maybe twenty feet wide. Obviously it was not a river, but it was wide enough to follow until it hopefully flowed into a bigger body of water or a river. Nightfall was enveloping him, but he was afraid to stop. He began following the flow of the water along the stream's bank. He kept slipping and tripping every few steps because of the darkness and the dampness of the bank. He tried moving further from the bank, but it didn't seem to get better. He found a bare path that seemed drier than the other areas. He thought it would be a good place to take a break and maybe even try to eat something.

He drank some water and sat down on his pack, now feeling the exhaustion overtake his adrenalin. His footing was poor, and continuing to push through the jungle in the dark was unsafe in many ways. He grabbed the rations and started eating whatever he reached. The rations didn't taste good or bad, but at least they didn't make him sick. At this point, he didn't care because he knew that he needed nourishment. He ate what he could and threw the rest back into the pack.

Tom was conscious enough to know that it wouldn't be safe sleeping on the ground this close to the water. He looked for a tree that he could climb that was thick enough to hold him and high enough so he would be hidden from the path and out of reach from any carnivorous animals that might be looking for a meal. He found a tree that looked strong enough. He strapped on his pack and weapon and started climbing. He reached about eight feet and hung his pack on a branch stump, and then he used his belt and ammo belt to secure himself to a trunk of the tree so he wouldn't fall when and if he fell asleep. He was exhausted, and as he began reviewing the day, he passed out, sound asleep.

His eyes remained closed, but he was conscious of birds and other jungle sounds. He could sense that it was no longer dark and that he was still in the tree and alive. He slowly opened his eyes to the predawn semilight, recognizing it was heavily overcast, with the clouds looking like rain at any moment. Tom surveyed the ground below his perch and began to unstrap himself. He lowered the pack down the tree and climbed to the damp ground. The sound of the stream was still nearby, so he continued to follow it down stream. The going was easier in the emerging daylight, but the slope of the bank was still wet and slippery. He moved to flatter ground and tried to keep a safe distance from the stream without separating himself too far from it. His hope remained that he was following the flow of water that would lead him to a river that would run into either an even bigger river or the sea.

Tom thought, *I'd rather be anywhere but here*! His mind continued to race even as he fought the heavy vegetation and rough terrain. Fear of being found by the Viet Cong, meaning capture or death, was still the controlling emotion, but the will to survive was also strong and driving his efforts.

As he cautiously continued along the stream, his thoughts turned to home and his family, wondering if he would ever see them again. He hadn't been the greatest son or even brother, plus he realized he wasn't a very good employee or student. His present circumstances were caused by his lack of commitment and failing to find more positives about his Army duties and assignment to Vietnam. His lack of effort and bad attitude now placed him in a life-and-death situation more dangerous than anything he had ever imagined. He committed to changing his approach to life if he was able to survive this grave challenge. He prayed that he would have the opportunity to make those changes.

5

Reality Gets Worse

THE SUN WAS helpless against the relentless thick gray clouds that blanketed the sky and covered the earth with a dull, colorless aura. Tom's negativity and feelings of helplessness absorbed his inner soul to the point of tears and thoughts of giving up.

Why me? Tom thought. *Was I really so bad they had to abandon me, knowing it would lead to my death? Even if the enemy doesn't find me, I could run out of food and likely catch pneumonia.*

With these thoughts, Tom realized how stupid and unlikely his plan for finding a river to float to safety really was. He felt that he may be better off being captured than continuing this hopeless trek. He was losing what little motivation he had and wallowing in his self-pity.

Regardless of what he thought and felt, he didn't stop because he knew he had to do something even if the plan was reckless and unattainable. He still had his weapons and some food, and there was no shortage of water. He kept up his slow but steady pace along the stream. He knew that he wasn't getting very far each day, but at least he kept moving. The stream was visible from his path along the top of the bank. The jungle continued to be thick with trees and brush as he made his own trail. Observing the stream, it seemed to be getting wider and even noisier. Maybe, just maybe, he was approaching the juncture of the stream with a river or at least a larger stream. He felt a brief twinge of optimism and pushed on.

Three days and nights of jungle, rain, clouds, and exhaustion brought him at least five miles from where he started. That wasn't very far, but Tom wasn't pushing himself too hard. Even though the stream continued to get wider and run quicker, he still had not heard the sounds of the river. He somehow managed to catch a squirrel, which he had to eat raw for obvious reasons. It was terrible and tough, but he knew his body needed the nutrients of the meat. It helped his spirit, as well as his strength. He stretched the meat for two meals, then, knowing it was probably going to rot, had to toss it. After killing and eating the squirrel, he at least knew he wasn't helpless and was surviving in this nightmare.

As he released his ropes on the fourth morning, he decided to check closer to the stream to see if anything was visible in its path. As he approached, he could see that

raw squirrel

the rains had swollen the stream, and loosened trees and branches were floating swiftly by him. He began to consider the risk of attempting to ride one of the tree trunks to speed up his journey. It had to be better than sloshing through the jungle. He noticed that the longer branches and trees were continuously getting stuck on the banks of the stream, so if he was going to do this, he would need a short but large tree trunk. He could keep his backpack and weapons on his back and shoulders to keep them reasonably dry, even though they were constantly watered by the unforgiving rain and mist. He waited and watched intently for the right float that could carry him but not get stuck on the bank. The best place to be was next to the stream. He inched his way down the steep bank, being cautious not to slip into the swift running waters.

He spotted a large log coming in the current and decided he had to give it a try. He strapped everything on tight, stepped into the stream, and caught the log. He straddled and lowered his weight onto it, making sure that the log could hold him. It seemed to work, although the bark was rough and slick. He found handholds on the trunk, and, with a deep breath and a silent prayer, he pushed off the bank and into the rushing water. The log was wobbling, and he strained to keep upright. He only had his hands and legs to steer and navigate, but it was working. He was totally focused on keeping afloat and keeping the log from hitting the bank. The swift current pushed him along quickly, much faster than his jungle struggles. He gained confidence in his steering and keeping upright, and, for a second time in the last couple of days, he felt positive about himself and his efforts to survive.

His journey on the log continued for several hours, and the stream continued to grow wider and probably deeper. A lot of debris was pushing down stream. He had to continuously push it away from his legs and his log. The log was proving to be a good vessel and was keeping him flowing steadily and swiftly with the stream's current.

As the stream winded through the jungle, Tom kept watching ahead for a possible river or signs of people or soldiers. Because of the size of the stream, he knew that there was the possibility of villages or military encampments along its path. The distinct roar of rushing water also began to reach his ear, increasing his hopes of finding the right body of water to take him South, back to American-controlled parts of Vietnam. Although he was in South Vietnam, he knew, as did every soldier, that the Viet Cong and North Vietnamese were everywhere, North and South.

He also knew that many soldiers and even sailors from the river boats had disappeared. They were either killed by the enemy and left to decompose, or they had been captured and subject to humiliation and torture, unlikely to survive at the hands of a heartless and ruthless enemy. Both of these outcomes weighed heavily on Tom's mind and spirit as he continued his quest for freedom.

6

Doing the Right Thing

Ned

IN THE MID-1960s, the Vietnam War was raging much worse than most Americans realized. The news about the conflict was limited until the late sixties when the battles and casualties began getting daily attention as it lingered on. Young men in high school began hearing about the draft and their potential to be called to duty. As they graduated high school and reached the age of eighteen, many chose to join the National Guard or reserve units to avoid being drafted into the Army or Marines. Others joined ROTC (Reserve Officers Training Corps) units with the Army or Navy in college so that they could continue in school, and they hoped that the war would be over by the time they finished. Unfortunately, that didn't work for many of them. Some of the young men became dedicated college students and received college deferments. Even conscientious objectors were drafted and placed in noncombative billets.

Many men followed their patriotic urgings and joined the various services, even volunteering for combat duty MOSs (military occupational specialty code) because they believed that was where they could best serve their country. Then there were other men who went to Canada or tried to find other excuses not to serve.

Ned joined the Naval ROTC (NROTC) while attending his state university. He was not opposed to serving in the military, but he wanted to finish his four-year degree before joining. He had set life goals for himself that would be delayed by his military service but would not keep him from his career as a financial analyst. He also planned to have a wife and children, live in New York City, and become a wealthy broker.

He attended drills, boot camp in the summer, as well as two weeks of training each year. As graduation approached, he began focusing more on what occupation he should sign up for after he transitioned to Naval active duty following graduation.

During his training, he had the opportunity to work with the Naval Intelligence Group, and the responsibility of that sector was very interesting to him. The group was likely made up of above-average individuals who he could learn from and would be good connections to communicate with after their military service. They were also out of harm's way at almost all their stations, and there were only a limited number even assigned to sea duty. He requested assignment to Naval Intelligence Group and it was approved.

He completed his degree in financial management with a very good 3.5 GPA. He had completed the first step to his professional future. He felt he was ready to fulfill his military obligation and then get on with his life as he had planned it out.

Ned would attend intelligence group officer training in Chicago and would be assigned to his first duty station from there. He completed the forms to apply for his security clearance. He attended schools for six months and had his Top Secret security clearance secured during that time. Approximately one month before graduation, orders were announced for Ned's graduating class.

Ned was confident that he would receive a quality duty station because he had finished at the top of his class. He was more concerned about sea duty because he wasn't sure how he would handle being aboard a ship for months at a time. He anxiously opened his envelope, read through the basic information, then read his assignment.

He slumped to his bunk and had to read it again because he could not believe what he read that he was being assigned to Naval Air Station in Da Nang, South Vietnam. He was going to be serving as the operations officer for the Naval Intelligence Group located at the air station. He would be the junior officer, and he envisioned he would do everything the unit needed done that the other officers didn't want to do. He would also have the opportunity to be part of a flight crew conducting communication services, and that was definitely an intriguing challenge. Another positive was that he would be promoted to LTJG (lieutenant junior grade) without serving the full year as was normally required.

Following graduation from officer training, he was given two weeks of leave, and then he would report to survival school in California. From there, he would fly from Travis AFB (Air Force Base) in California, then directly to Da Nang to begin his assignment. It was a twelve-month assignment. That was the normal tour for Naval officers assigned to Vietnam.

Leaving his family and friends was traumatic, as they all knew where he was going. His mom hugged him fiercely, burying her head in his chest. "You come back to me," she said through her tears. "Promise me."

Ned patted her back as he fought emotion of his own. "You don't need to worry. I have a safe assignment." He gently pushed her back, so they could make eye contact. "Besides, I'll have a Marine assigned to me. If there's any chance of my getting captured, he'll just shoot me!" Instead of lightening the mood like Ned had hoped, the joke was too morbid, and fresh tears threatened. Unable to maintain eye contact with her, he looked up and was shocked to see the tears in his father's eyes.

Never a man of many words, Ned's father clamped him on the shoulder and said, "I'm proud of you, son."

Ned wiped a tear that had escaped off his cheek, hoping no one else at the airport saw it. He was going to war; he was supposed to be strong now.

"This is the final boarding call," a soft voice called out.

The small family embraced one last time. Ned took a deep breath to steady himself, full of determination to fulfill his duty.

"We'll see each other again soon," he promised.

He grabbed his luggage and walked off to his fate, taking one last look at his father supporting his mother as she cried into her hands.

Survival school was a challenge he hadn't properly prepared himself for, but he made it through. It was five days of misery, learning hand-to-hand combat, the enemy's tactics what to expect when they arrived in country, and how to survive on his own in a desolate and hostile environment. Their stateside Naval uniforms were replaced with fatigues and combat footwear. Even their hats were now green, officers and enlisted alike. The survival training was a confidence builder for all who attended because they believed that they were now better prepared to enter the theater of war that they had all heard about. Although the training had been difficult, Ned had made it through.

After survival training, Ned traveled to San Francisco to spend his last night in the states before boarding at Travis. Fortunately, most of the other survival school graduates were also going to Vietnam. They gathered at a bar in San Francisco and threw one last massive drinking party together.

Ned wasn't a big drinker, but he kept up as long as he could before passing out. He awoke the next morning in his room extremely sick. He had no idea how he got there, but he was glad someone was watching out for him and got him back. It was a miserable trip to Travis on the military bus, but most of the other passengers were feeling the same. Obviously it was a quiet trip.

His hangover put him to sleep for most of the trip, even though there were frequent trips to the bathroom for multiple purposes.

About four hours from landing, Ned awoke and began thinking about what was ahead. He hoped he was ready to perform up to the level of excellence that was expected of a young officer. Because his job had not been well defined, he wondered what his duties would be. He tried to envision what kind of enemy activity there was near his duty station and his living quarters. He pondered about a lot of things that could only be answered when he got there. He was worried, fearful, and excited at one time.

As the passengers deplaned, Ned started looking for his connection. A lieutenant approached him at the bottom of the steps and asked, "What's your name, Lieutenant?"

He saluted the LT and stated, "LT(jg) Ned, sir!" and gave the lieutenant his orders.

The lieutenant introduced himself as Jeff Scott. "I'm the Executive Officer for the Naval Intelligence unit." After reviewing the orders, LT Scott led Ned to a jeep, and they proceeded to a hut on the far side of the airport runways. Planes were constantly landing and taking off, and Ned thought it was remarkable how they kept from colliding.

They entered the small hut where there were several desks and file cabinets crammed into the limited space. There were three enlisted men and two other officers. They introduced themselves, then Jeff took him into a small office in the back of the hut, the Commanding Officer's office.

LT Scott introduced Commander Bill Shank, referring to him as Captain. Mr. Shank invited Ned to sit in his one extra chair, and LT Scott departed and closed the door behind him.

After Ned answered Captain Shank's questions about his background and education, the captain began to explain to Ned what the mission and duties of the unit were. He said, "Ned, this unit has been in existence less than a year in Da Nang. There is a second intelligence unit in Saigon. This unit is committed to communication security using the AWAC or Airborne Warning and Control System planes parked outside the hut. There is also a small unit located at the Marine base in Phu Bai, fifty miles to the northwest. Everyone does everything because we are such a small unit with a lot of responsibilities. Your primary responsibility will initially be to serve as the duty officer with one of the flight crews, as well as be the security officer for the unit."

Ned was pleased with this assignment because he was anxious to be a part of the flight crew. The security assignment would be fine, other than the occasional trips he would have to make to Phu Bai and Saigon. The more Captain Shank talked, the more Ned realized the importance of this group's mission, how it affected military security and the ground troops across the Vietnam countryside. There were also members of this unit assigned to riverboats on the major rivers, as well as Marine units, clearly dangerous places to be. His appreciation for his unit members grew significantly. He hoped he could match their courage.

Ned was taken to the other Quonset hut next to the operations center by LT Scott. It served as the living quarters for everyone in the unit. He chose a bunk and a couple of empty lockers. His shipmates informed him about the schedules, where they had chow, when the officers' club was, and other important information. His shipmates were talkative, very open and friendly, which was great for Ned. There wasn't a big deal about who was enlisted and who was an officer. They only had themselves, and they were interdependent.

The first evening, the other officers took him to the officers' club for dinner and drinks. Their backgrounds were similar because they all had joined NROTC so that they could complete their degrees before beginning their active service. The officers came from varied locations across the United States, including New York, Georgia, and California, as well as points in between. Ned knew he was with the right group of people for his military time, as well as his future afterward. It was a relaxed enjoyable evening, but he avoided overdrinking because he didn't want to repeat the San Francisco experience. The food was surprisingly good, but the drinks didn't taste too good for some reason.

Before going to the club, they had taken him to the bank to switch his US currency for Vietnamese piasters (or dong—money). American currency was the biggest black-market item, so any US money had to be exchanged. Even in the on-base stores and clubs, the Vietnamese workers would attempt to keep the US currency because of its value on the black market.

The next day, thanks to not drinking much, Ned had a clear head, and he began learning his duties from his fellow officers. He understood that the unit was relatively new and that the duties and responsibilities were still being defined.

His read a lot of the manuals that described the mission and objectives of the unit, as well as the explanations for each job duty. His best learning came from shadowing his fellow officers and working with the enlisted people, performing the real duties of their assignments, not just the written description.

He jumped in, anxious to learn and contribute. He began to learn the personalities of his fellow shipmates and their backgrounds and why they were here. His appreciation for them continued to grow, and he learned more about them. His job required a lot of concentration because of the level of security information the unit dealt with.

Ned's first flight assignment was the next day, and he was definitely looking forward to it. As much as he anticipated the flight, it was actually uneventful. Learning the functions of the AWAC and its equipment was very informative. A few weeks later, he made his first trip to Phu Bai with LT Scott via helicopter. He was very nervous on this trip, not only because of the low flight level of the copter but also flying into a combat area that wasn't far from the DMZ (or so it was called). The flight crew was not part of the security group but was attached to the Naval air unit at Da Nang. They were normally assigned to transporting people back and forth to the ships offshore. Unfortunately, many of them were seriously wounded.

While the helicopter flew over different areas, one of the crew members said, "There have been many battles fought in the jungles below, and we have been in and out of it many times, more times than we want to remember. There has been a lot of damage inflicted by both sides, each winning some and losing some." After listening to what the crew member had said, Ned thought, *This is interesting information but rather morbid.*

He could see areas where the ground was heavily cratered from mortars and artillery shellings and he could only imagine how much blood had been shed by soldiers from both sides wounded or even losing their lives in the now unoccupied areas.

This trip was also uneventful. They landed safely at Phu Bai, made an exchange with the Intelligence Group officer, then went back on the copter for the return trip to Da Nang.

Ned settled into a routine along with the rest of the crew. As he continued to gain confidence, he was assigned more responsibilities, which kept his job interesting and challenging. There was no problem with boredom, and his shipmates kept everyone from being too lonely. If anyone started to isolate themselves or drinking too much or any other signs of possible problems, the shipmates intervened and brought that individual back into the fold. This group was tight, and they couldn't allow any of the members to weaken or fail. That wasn't acceptable! The pride of the unit kept the standards high and the teamwork optimum.

7

Enemy Fire

NED'S FLIGHT CREW rotated to fly every third day, and he continued to enjoy this duty the best. Even though the trips were normally without incident, it was just the sense of how meaningful the work was and the value to the military it provided. Likewise, the trips to Phu Bai, which he now did on his own once per week, became more routine, and while meaningful, they were, thankfully, also uneventful.

After he had been in country six months, Captain Shank asked him, "Ned, are you interested in extending your Vietnam assignment for an additional six months or a year? If you choose to extend, you will be eligible for an extra thirty-day leave once you have completed a year, and your active duty requirement will be reduced by the length of the extension."

Ned asked, "Will my assignment stay the same, or will I be required to move or change positions?"

Captain Shank replied, "Ned, I can assure you that because I am pleased with your performance, I am looking forward to having you in my command for as long as you are willing to stay."

After reflecting on all the positives and negatives, Ned decided it was worth the extension to get his active duty requirement reduced. He doubted that he would decide to make the Navy his career, so getting out and starting his civilian career sooner than expected would be a great opportunity. He decided to extend for one year, thus being able to cash in on all the incentives that came with the extension; he was especially excited about the extra thirty days at home.

Soon after he had signed his extension, the infamous TET Offensive by the North Vietnamese began. It was bad enough that it was monsoon season, but to have the airfield bombed every night, plus the massive increase in troop activity, kept the Intelligence Group very busy and very tired. They kept up analyzing everything they collected and then distributed, but the intensity and stress were at times unbearable. Phu Bai was constantly under attack from Viet Cong troops and missile batteries. Damage was extensive, and replacement equipment was continuously being flown in; injuries and fatalities were significant, so replacements were also being transported daily. This was Ned's and most of his unit members' first experience with TET, so it was scary and maddening. They wished they could do more to fight the enemy. They committed to doing the best at what they were responsible for, keeping everyone as up to date as possible with the information they needed.

The weather sometimes prevented AWAC missions from taking off, but they fought through as often as possible, taking greater risks than they should have. Their commitment to duty was greater than their fear of the risk. The takeoffs and landings were rough, but the information collected could be very useful to fight back the enemy. It was worth it to everyone involved, and the unit grew closer together because of it.

The courier trips to Phu Bai were also reduced because of the activity around it and the weather. But whenever possible, the trips were made because the information was critical to the war effort. On a relatively clear day, Ned volunteered to make a trip to Phu Bai, and it was approved. The helicopter pilot and copilot were the same guys who had flown him and LT Jeff on his first mission to Phu Bai, so he was looking forward to the conversations and stories they would tell.

The trip to Phu Bai was relatively smooth and no enemy fire was received. The two pilots and Ned were thankful and hoped the return trip would be similarly uneventful. Ned did the document exchange, loading the new information into his satchel. He had a brief visit with the intelligence officer and checked on his need for equipment or supplies.

Thus far, even with all the enemy activity, the security unit had not experienced any serious injuries, just some minor cuts and bruises from missile barrages. All the other supplies were unloaded and the copter refueled, ready for the return trip to Da Nang. The skies were cloudy, but no severe weather was predicted. The pilots and Ned donned their flak jackets and helmets and then checked their weapons, just in case. Ned was mentally thankful that he had two well-experienced pilots transporting him, knowing they had seen a lot of this war in the worst possible places. They were the best he could possibly ask for.

Less than twenty miles out of Phu Bai, Ned started hearing the sound of missile and mortar batteries firing. He looked out the door window and could see the smoke from the missiles in the near distance. Suddenly he felt and heard the front of the copter being hit, jerking all three of them almost out of their seats. The foot controls were damaged. It was still flyable, but probably with limited range.

The pilot immediately sent an SOS message to Da Nang and Phu Bai, knowing that the copter would likely have to land before reaching Da Nang, and they would have to be picked up. Just as the SOS was sent, another missile scraped the bottom of the copter, sending metal from the floorboard all through the cockpit. All three of them were hit, with the hot shrapnel painfully piercing their skin. This hit affected the balance of the copter, and the pilots had to begin trying to manually keep the wounded machine airborne and moving toward safety.

As the machine lost altitude, they began receiving ground fire, bullets spraying throughout the cockpit. Ned could only helplessly watch as the copilot was hit multiple times, at least one of them fatal. The pilot began to look for a landing spot that was close and would perhaps give them a chance to defend themselves. Ned marveled at the pilot who, in spite of his wounds, kept focused, and identified a hill about two miles away. Ned could only think to shoot back at where he thought the enemy was firing from. He even threw several grenades that were in the ammo box, hoping to hit a mortar or missile battery, anything to reduce the enemy fire. He had only received several scrapes from the small arms shelling, but the shrapnel wounds were much more painful, but he had to fight through it.

The copter kept bouncing and swerving, almost out of the pilot's control. He was doing a remarkable job of keeping it aloft. As they neared his planned landing spot, he dumped the fuel from the tanks, hoping to avert an explosion or fire when they hit.

The ground fire continued, and there was even less protection as they continued to lose altitude. Ned began to sense that they were getting past the enemies firing at them, so perhaps they would be out of range soon. As he thought this, another barrage hit them, this time hitting the pilot numerous times.

Ned was struck in his shoulder, but again, it wasn't serious. His flak jacket and helmet deflected what would have been serious, likely fatal, shots. Sadly, the neck hits that the pilot received were going to cost him his life soon. The badly damaged copter continued in its very limited capacity toward a rather high hill with rocks at the top. The pilot began to succumb to his multiple wounds, but he wanted to give Ned an opportunity to survive in spite of the bad odds. Blood ran profusely from his neck and began to pool up in his seat. His vision was total blurred and going dark he made one last adjustment and placed the copter down as gently as he could on to the ground. He closed his eyes and slumped over, doing his duty heroically until the end.

Ned survived the crash with only a sprained ankle from the landing. He also had the bullet wounds and several painful shrapnel wounds, but he was still able to crawl out of the wreckage. Thankfully there was no fire, and the most damage was caused by the enemy weapons and not the crash landing.

He quickly surveyed the area around the crash, hoping to find shelter for protection nearby. He had limited mobility, but he had no idea where he was. Ned didn't want to get too far from the wreckage because he had to get supplies and the bodies of the pilots out of it.

There was a natural formation of rocks near the top of the hill but close to the wreckage, and it was his best opportunity for safety as well as cover. He knew that as a courier, his first responsibility was to protect the satchel of documents he had brought from Phu Bai. He placed the package into the rocks so it was out of sight and protected from any inclement weather. Ned then pulled the bodies of the two pilots from the wreckage and dragged them into the rock formation. He was not going to let the enemy desecrate or steal their bodies. They were heroes in his eyes, and he intended to protect them until they were all rescued. Even though it wasn't burning now, he was also concerned that the copter might ignite without warning.

Unfortunately, the crash happened late in the day, and Ned anticipated that he would have to spend a night in hiding, waiting for the search teams the next day. Viet Cong search teams would also be looking for the wreckage to seek any useable weapons or equipment and any survivors they could capture. The North Vietnamese paid substantially for American captives, especially officers.

He committed himself to not getting captured and to protect the bodies of the pilots. He knew this would mean fighting to his death if necessary, but he feared capture more than dying in battle.

Ned collected all the weapons from the wrecked copter, including three M16s and three .45s, with four ammo clips for each. There were also four grenades that he thought might be useful. It wasn't much, but it was all he could find. He also took the small supply of water and some ration boxes. Loading everything into the rocks near the wreckage, he set up his observation angles to watch for enemies advancing. Thankfully he was near the top of a hill, making observation easier. Remarkably, the copter wreckage was not burning or even smoking, so it wasn't an easy find for Viet Cong patrols, especially when it became dark.

8

Fear, Pain, and Mission

NED TRIED TO apply first aid to his wounds and his sprained ankle. He washed out the ones he could reach, but several pieces were stuck in his upper back and not reachable. He wrapped the ankle as tightly as he could with gauze, and that seemed to give him some support. The shrapnel and gunshot wounds were more painful, but he knew he had to keep his head focused on the situation to protect his documents and the bodies of the two pilots.

He collected his thoughts, recalled what had happened in the last fifteen minutes, and anticipated what was yet to come. Reality set in.

He was scared to death.

As the sun was setting, he could hear a vehicle coming closer. He peered through the rocks to see a small pickup with four men in various forms of uniforms mixed with their Vietnamese clothing approaching the wreckage. As they drew closer, he could see they were armed, likely with AK-47s, and looking intently at the wreckage, watching for any movement or signs of life.

Ned had a decision to make. He thought, *Should I stay in hiding and hope that they search the wreckage and don't look in the surrounding area, or do I stand and fight, hoping to kill or wound all four of the enemy before they hit me?*

Knowing what was at stake with the classified information and the bodies of the pilots, he decided he didn't really have a choice but to stand and fight. Nothing in his life so far could have prepared him for these circumstances or the decisions he would have to make.

Ned was an office dweller, had never been in combat, and had never fired a weapon at another human being. He had been a good marksman in basic, but that was at targets; plus, his hands, arms, and upper body weren't shaking profusely in basic training. He was now faced with a life-and-death situation when all his training would have to overcome all his fear.

He thought about home and his family, the real possibility of never seeing them again, or being left on the battle field, never to be found. But he had only seconds to consider anything; the enemy soldiers were approaching the wreckage, which was only ten yards or so from his hiding spot. As the enemy reached the wreckage and saw there was no life in or around it, they let their weapons down in order to search the wreckage for useable supplies or equipment. Their interest was on salvaging. They would search the area for the survivors after they looted the helicopter.

Ned knew that he had only one chance, one opportunity to hit them all. If he wasn't accurate, he would be dead. The evening light was giving way to darkness, making it more critical to act quickly. He checked the clip on the M16. It was a double clip, so he could do two quick bursts with only a quick flip of the clip. Ned tried to remember where the safety was on or off. He couldn't have that factor cause a fail.

He steadied himself as well as he could and watched the movements of the four Viet Cong scavengers. He had to have all four visible at the same time to pull this off. Each of them was dipping in and out of the wreckage, pulling out usable items and laying them on the ground in a pile that they would then stack in the pickup truck.

Ned noticed they would usually talk after each trip to the truck, then return to the wreckage together. As they completed their trip to the truck and began to return to the downed copter, he said a prayer, took a deep breath, flipped the safety, leveled the M16 on a rock, sighted in the first scavenger, and began to fire. The M16 was smooth and true, clearing the first clip quickly. One of the scavengers raised his rifle to return fire, but Ned shot him before he could squeeze the trigger.

Ned didn't know how, but all four scavengers went down. He flipped the clip and waited, watching for any movement from the four bodies. There was none. He left the protection of the rocks and approached the bodies. There was still no movement as he reached the first. He kept the M16 on the ready, prepared to fire with any signs of life. He poked each body with the barrel of his rifle, and there was no response or movement. Just to be sure, he reached down to check the pulse on each. There was none for any of them. He had done it. Ned began to shake profusely, and tears filled his eyes. His heart was thumping in his throat and chest. He vomited violently. He was suddenly sad, mad, fearful, but yet very thankful to be alive. He had taken four lives but had performed his mission of protecting the classified material and kept the bodies of the pilots away from the enemies' desecration. But he wasn't done. His first thought was to load the bodies of the pilots and his satchel, along with the weapons, and attempt to drive to safety. He then realized this was not realistic because he had no idea where he was. He only knew that he was in enemy territory, and his chances of being captured or killed were much greater if he attempted to drive away.

Instead, he decided to figure out how to dispose of the truck and bodies before their comrades came searching for them. The empty truck and dead bodies would make survivor presence apparent. He dragged the bodies back to the truck and pulled three of them into the bed. He started the truck and moved it so it was pointed down the hill but away from the direction it had come from. He then loaded the last body into the driver's seat, draping the corpse's arms through the openings in the steering wheel to keep the truck from turning. He started the truck, put the body's foot on the accelerator so it was racing the engine, then he forced the truck into gear. The truck lurched and jerked ahead, speeding down the hill. He watched as the truck careened and lurched, building up speed until it disappeared into the jungle at the bottom of the hill. He expected to hear an explosion, but instead, he saw a small plume of smoke and no flames within the jungle's grasp.

The smoke didn't seem to last very long, and it was almost indistinguishable because of the darkness. He estimated the truck must have stopped about a mile from the helicopter's wreckage. He hoped that it was far enough that his hiding spot wouldn't be suspected as the origination of the truck.

Ned knew he was far from safe, and other patrols would likely come around before he was rescued. It was now completely dark except for the light of the quarter moon, which wasn't much illumination for keeping watch.

He returned to the relative safety of his shelter and began to recount the happenings of the day. He didn't want to, but his mind raced through each item, starting with his hangover and lack of breakfast. It was the scariest, most painful, worst day of his life. He had been forced to make decisions he thought he would never have to make, performing duties he believed were beyond his capabilities, facing his greatest fears, and having regrets he would have never imagined and would likely haunt him for the rest of his life.

His emotions were racing, and he wondered if he would have the ability, the courage, and the levelheadedness to kill again if another enemy patrol approached the wreckage.

The pain from his multiple wounds began to intensify. Even though there was morphine in the emergency medical kit, he was afraid to use it because it may put him to sleep or groggy. This would render him helpless if another patrol came.

He checked the boxes of K rations and found a can of chicken and noodles, his favorite. He ate them and a cookie. He took a small drink of water, wanting to conserve what he had left just in case he wasn't rescued soon, which was his biggest fear next to being killed or captured.

He continuously checked the perimeter, with no movement seen. The only noise coming from the jungle sounds in the distance. He decided he would risk smoking a cigarette from the K-rats box. To play it safe, he covered his head with his shirt so that when he lit the match, it wouldn't illuminate the darkness surrounding his position.

The cigarette tasted fantastic, and he thought, *Smoking some good pot would be so good right now.* He finished the smoke and thoroughly extinguished it before pulling his shirt from over his head, then immediately surveyed the perimeter again. He could faintly smell the lingering smoke from the cigarette, and he hoped it would not reach beyond the wreckage site.

As he scanned the jungle for movement and unusual noises, he decided that he was fairly safe for now. Ned committed to staying vigilant all night, understanding the severity of his situation. He remained in the total darkness of the shelter, putting on a light coat under his flak jacket to protect himself against the nighttime chill. He scanned from side to side to observe the entire perimeter, slowly observing as best he could in the darkness.

He resolved to fight until he had nothing left to give. He checked his weapons, changing the clip in the M16 weapon to a full double. The .45 was loaded and on his hip. Thankfully he had more than one weapon, so if one failed, he had a backup. He didn't have much ammunition, but at least he had weapons.

Ned didn't consider himself a fighter or a warrior, but they were going to have to kill him before he killed the enemy. Ned's fear began to change to anger. He thought about why he was in this circumstance and raged against the Viet Cong who shot down the helicopter. *I am so angry at my commanding officer in NROTC, who recommended I try for the intelligence unit because they seldom were placed in harm's way. What a crock that has turned out to be.*

He also became angry at himself for not paying closer attention in basic and then in survival school so he would be better prepared to face his current situation. He certainly could have been more focused at the firing range so he would understand how to better sight the M16 and how he was supposed to take care of it. He had blown through a lot of ammunition to kill the four Viet Cong scavengers, and he knew he couldn't keep doing that with his limited supply. He thought of what he would miss if he was killed—the friendships, the opportunities he had planned for when he got out of the military, maybe a wife and kids, a career, and, hopefully, wealth. It was a future that now seemed unattainable.

His mind was racing as he sat on a rock within the meager shelter he was hoping would keep him safe as long as possible. He tried to remember how to pray, but the words escaped him. All he could do was talk to God. He said, "God, I ask you to please forgive me for not making You part of my life and for all the bad things I have done. If possible, I ask you to help me out of this mess. I pray that you will give me the courage and fortitude to handle whatever happens." It was all he could think to say at that moment, but he repeated it several times. As he thought these words, his mind drifted, and without realizing it, he could not keep his eyes open.

He jerked awake when his head fell out of his hands, and he almost fell to the ground. It was still dark, so he looked at his watch and saw that he had only slept a couple of hours. Fear again overtook him, thinking enemy patrols or scavengers may be present at or nearing the wreckage. He quickly jumped up and immediately fell to the ground pain because he had forgotten about his sprained ankle and the shrapnel in his back. It was going to be rough doing what he needed to do, but he had no choice.

This time, he rose to his feet slowly and went to his lookout points. He checked all around his shelter and saw that nothing appeared different from before he passed out. He looked at the wreckage area and found nothing varied from earlier in the night. Ned cursed himself for falling asleep. Fear, again, was his primary emotion, along with hopelessness, self-pity, and pain. He concluded that his likely outcome was either dying from an enemy bullet or from blood poisoning from his wounds. He had no idea if the SOS sent by the pilot had been received or if rescue teams would even come for him. He felt more alone than ever before.

9

Another Threat

H IS WATCH SHOWED 0530 as first light began to appear in the east. There wasn't enough to thoroughly observe his surroundings. The sky was filled with low clouds, producing a steady miserable mist. The jungle noises were the same but with more birds singing now.

He looked down the hill where he had steered the pickup and could not see it or any smoke coming from it. He still thought that was strange. He knew that the small groups of Viet Cong operated on their own and had only occasional communication with other units or the North Vietnamese, so he wasn't surprised that no one had come looking for the four scavengers. He did think other patrols would have been searching for the helicopter's wreckage by now, but he was thankful that they hadn't been. The path where the pickup had approached was empty, although he could only see about five hundred yards before it was swallowed by the jungle brush. He relaxed slightly and realized he was very hungry.

Searching through the K-rats, he found enough likeable items to get him going. He drank some water but continued to conserve. His nerves were tingling, his mind was racing, and the combination of fear and anger were controlling him. He slowly walked around as if he was pacing the floor, continuously looking out of the shelter's sides so that he would not miss any movement or any noise changes.

Above the din of the jungle noises, he heard mumbled sound of voices, and they were slowly getting louder and more distinguishable. He knew it wasn't American voices, and as the words became more distinct, the language expressed was clearly Vietnamese.

He hunched over and went to the edge of his shelter, peering out in the direction of the voices. He could make out two people approaching and talking to one another. They were at least one hundred yards away.

As they drew closer, he recognized them as two young men armed with older versions of the AK-47 slung across their shoulders. They were heading directly for the wreckage. It was apparent they weren't too concerned with the possibility of survivors. They were obviously only interested in looting whatever the copter wreckage had of value or they could use in their huts, maybe even items they could trade.

Ned had to again make a quick decision as they approached. If he shot them, the noise of his weapon may draw the attention of others; if he let them check the wreckage and take items from it, they may search further and find him in the shelter of rocks. He knew he couldn't fight them hand to hand because he had no experience or even training on how to fight or kill someone using a knife or any other hand weapon. He could take the risk of letting them pillage the wreckage and hope they would leave without searching further. Then he thought of another option, including how he could use the two bodies if he went ahead and shot them. Knowing other patrols would likely be coming to check the wreckage, he thought he could take the two bodies and place them in the pilot and copilot seats, strap them in, and place the helmets on their heads. If patrols checked the inside of the cockpit, they would see two bodies where there should be and think there were no survivors. This would give Ned more time to prepare and defend himself. He wished he would have thought about this when the first four scavengers had been there.

After weighing his options, he determined that he would need to take the risk of gunfire to kill the two Vietnamese who were approaching and place them in the copter seats to masquerade as the two pilots. He would need to again act and fire quickly, hoping to use a minimum amount of ammunition, not only to conserve them but to keep from making excessive noise that would likely attract unwelcomed attention. He knew he had to do this or risk being found and killed by the two scavengers.

As the two reached the wreckage, they began walking around it to check for anything worth taking. Ned saw his opportunity when they came close to the entry to his shelter. He fired one shot, hitting the first enemy in the head. His second shot hit the second man in the chest. Neither made a sound, moving only slightly before dying from Ned's bullets.

They fell near the copter's door, making it easier for Ned to wrestle them into the pilots' seats. He finally managed to get them placed in the seats and then covered their heads with the helmets. From the outside of the copter, only the helmet was visible through the windows. This made it more unlikely for the enemy to identify them as non-Americans.

He crawled back to the shelter, totally exhausted and again experiencing a burst of different emotions. He had completed his objective, and he felt like he had added an element to his defenses. As tired and emotional as he felt, he knew he had to remain vigilant because other patrols were sure to approach the wreckage. He had to hold out until the rescuers could find him.

10

Overrun

As the sun continued its rise into the dreary, overcast sky, Ned surveyed his perimeter and the paths leading to it. Being at the top of this hill gave him a definite advantage to spot anyone who might be approaching. Thankfully it was still all clear. He wondered again if the SOS had gotten through and if there would be rescue crews looking for him. Unfortunately, the weather was typical for monsoon: overcast, low sky, and a steady mist. It was definitely not good flying weather. With everything else going on, the weather just contributed to his feelings of hopelessness. He decided that he had to try to eat something, so he pilfered through the ration boxes and found enough food items to satisfy what little appetite he had. He took a larger-than-usual gulp of water, thinking, *What am I keeping it for anyway?* Plus, with the blood loss, he needed to replace fluids as much as possible. He knew that he was very tired, sore, and afraid. Because of the mist, he was also feeling very cold. He couldn't do anything about those things except call on his training and have the will to live and push back on the negative feelings and thoughts that were trying to overwhelm him.

He began to think about the two enemy encounters that he had and how he mustered the courage to confront the enemy and shoot other human beings. He couldn't justify taking other's lives, but it was either kill-or-be-killed situations. He hoped and prayed there would not be any more of those situations. It was interesting that since his conversation with God, he felt some type of connection to him, although he didn't understand how that was possible. Right now, it seemed to make sense to include God in his thoughts. That reflection actually gave him some comfort.

The outline of the sun began to peak over the horizon but was engulfed in the clouds and did not beam much light and definitely no heat. His doubts about the possibility of a quick rescue grew even more. He began to feel that he would be called upon to defend himself and the bodies of the pilots before rescuers arrived. He was also worried about infection spreading, causing more issues. He knew he had to stay focused on the here and now, keeping a vigilant watch for possible enemy patrols approaching. Ned checked his weapons and ammunition. He hadn't used the .45s, so they were still ready. He had concealed the ammunition and .45s, plus the two extra M16s in between the rocks to keep them as dry as possible. He had used all of one clip and only two shells from another for the M16s, so he had two full double clips, one full clip, and one minus two. Not much but he committed to conserving and making it last as long as possible, if the need arose. He placed a .45 and an extra M16 close to his best observation point in the shelter.

The hill dropped off severely on what he considered the back side, so he did not suspect an enemy approaching from there. The front side was not as steep, and several paths were visible from his one best vantage point. In spite of the various directions, he believed he could adjust enough to defend himself if they approached from any of the paths. Again he hoped none of this preparation was necessary, but he had to be prepared and stay vigilant. His mind kept rolling quickly from thought to thought, so many that they only entered for a moment, then were replaced by another. He gave up trying to concentrate on one and just let his thoughts to flow on.

He had to keep his physical awareness on his mission, staying awake and not giving in to fear. He had to overcome the conditions and the feelings that he was experiencing. It would be so great if this was all just a bad dream and he would be waking up soon. It would also be great if he heard the sound of a helicopter approaching. Either would be such a miracle!

As his mind continued to race, he thought he heard the faint sound of a vehicle. He surveyed the perimeter and couldn't see anything out of the ordinary. The sound became more distinct, and it became clearer that it was a motor vehicle that was getting closer. He watched the paths, trying to anticipate which one the vehicle was approaching on, even though only one of them appeared to be wide enough for a regular vehicle.

The volume of the vehicle continued to increase, sounding more like it was approaching on the same path the pickup had approached from yesterday. To his dismay, he thought that he could actually hear two similar vehicles drawing closer. From the jungle foliage, a jeep became visible, and a second jeep was following.

As the jeeps approached the wreckage, Ned could make out probably five or six people in each. There was a machine gun mounted on the top of both of the jeeps, manned by a gunner at the ready. The other occupants were clearly heavily armed as well.

The hair on the back of his neck was standing on end, and his skin tingled with cold chills. His aim would have to be even more accurate than in the previous two encounters, and he would have to be mindful of his ammo supply. His odds were not good.

The unexpected then happened as the jeeps drew closer. One of them turned off, actually following the approximate path that the pickup had followed when Ned directed it down the side of the hill. He briefly thought maybe the odds weren't so totally against him.

The first jeep pulled up to the wreckage, and what looked like the leader, perhaps an officer, got out and glanced at the cockpit. He saw the two helmets atop the pilots' seats, turned and said something to the others, and they all laughed.

Ned thought, *Perhaps the masquerade worked.*

The other soldiers climbed out, except for the gunner on top, and began milling about the wreckage. A couple of them started looking around the area, taking extended looks at the rocks. Ned felt that he was out of their sight lines but also knew he would need to act, especially considering that the second jeep would likely return soon. His odds were as good as they were going to get. He strategized his moves: take out the jeep gunner first, then the officer, then the farthest from him to the closest. That way, they had less chance to run or seek shelter. He would single fire as long as he was hitting them but would switch to bursts if he needed to. He definitely didn't want to because it would blow through his ammo. If this worked, he could pick up some of their AK-47s and their ammo, which would keep him going even longer. First things first.

He took a deep breath, steadied his nerves as best he could, sighted in on the gunner, and squeezed the trigger twice. Without waiting to see the results, he swung his M16 to the officer, who was just looking up, and fired at his head, again firing twice, then swung to the right and fired at the next farthest, then the next, and so on until he had fired at all six.

He looked back across his range of fire and saw that all six enemies had been hit. He wasn't sure how seriously their wounds were. The jeep gunner was slumped down into the jeep, and Ned felt confident that he was not conscious. The officer was flat on the ground in a large pool of blood, and so were two others. The two closest to him were crawling toward their weapons, even though they were definitely wounded.

Ned's only choice was to shoot them again. This time, he used the .45 because he was close enough not to miss, and he needed to save the M16 ammo. He did not want the enemy soldiers to suffer (he didn't know why he thought about it, but he did), so he aimed for and struck each of them in the head, killing them instantly. He was thankful his aim was true but hadn't remembered how much the .45 would kick. He could not believe how accurate his aim was with the M16 and the .45.

He knew that he had to move as quickly as he could because the other jeep likely heard the shooting and would be racing back to the wreckage. He ran out as fast as he could and grabbed the two enemy soldier's rifles and their ammo clips. He then scurried back to the shelter and prepared for the next attack. There would be no surprising this next group, and they would know there were survivors who were fighting back, although they may not know where they were hiding.

The enemy also didn't know that the survival list was only one person, and he was glad they didn't. Ned had to develop his strategy even more quickly this time because they were sure to be there within seconds. He recalled that he had saved the four grenades from the copter and thought now would be a good time to make use of them. He didn't have much of a pitching arm, but with him being so fearful, he felt he could throw a grenade a mile.

He thought, *I am going to shoot the jeep's gunner, throw two grenades as quickly as possible into the path of the jeep, and hope they explode at just the right time to destroy the jeep and at least injure all the occupants.* He would then use the AK-47s in rapid fire, since he had more ammunition for them, to hopefully kill the enemy who were still moving.

Ned was again shaking uncontrollably, but he knew he had to collect himself quickly. He grabbed a quick shot of water, yelled at his aching wounds, and set himself in position for the return of the enemy.

He needed the clearest line of sight to the path the jeep would be returning on, so he moved where the copter wreckage so it did not block his view. He placed each weapon within his reach, including the .45 that he had reloaded with a fresh clip. Three to go, he thought. Surprisingly, the day was becoming brighter and clearer. The cloud cover was much higher, and the clouds seemed thinner. The mist had stopped for the moment. He felt a twang of optimism, thinking maybe the rescue crews could still get here in time. It was a nice thought, but he had to stay in the present, the here and now, or it could cost him his life.

He heard the faint murmur of the jeep beginning its ascent up the hill, back to the wreckage. The noise of the engine grew louder as the jeep struggled up the hill. He could see them about a hundred yards away and began sighting in on the gunner, who was sticking out the top of the jeep. He had to make the first shots very true to their mark for the rest of his plan to work.

He reached down to verify that the two grenades were within his grasp. The jeep began speeding up as it got to the flatter part of the hill. When it was about twenty-five yards out, he pressed the trigger three times, threw the AK-47 down, grabbed the first grenade, pulled the pin, took a quick look at the jeep, and let it go.

Without waiting for the results, he repeated his grenade routine, this time having a closer throw because of the jeep's approach. As he let go of the second one, the first one exploded, lifting the rear of the jeep off the ground and blowing parts all over the place. The second one ignited in the front, scattering jeep parts in a giant radius and throwing the jeep onto its side. The gas tank exploded from the first grenade, and soon the jeep was totally engulfed with flames.

Ned could see three occupants jump out. Unfortunately, one had his clothes on fire. He shot him first to keep him from suffering, then he aimed at the other two with the AK, shooting on burst to have a better chance of hitting them.

He felt severe burning sensations in his side and back, all the way up to his neck. He failed to notice one of the other occupants rolling out of the jeep, which was on its back side, to throw a grenade into the shelter. It landed and then exploded only eight feet from Ned. That soldier started firing at Ned, hitting his helmet several times, and his shoulder. The pain was unbelievable. It was not a bone-crushing wound, so he had to persevere and fight on.

He quickly swung his aim to the soldier firing at him and hit him several times. The first two were also wounded, but they were returning fire. He checked for others and, seeing none, concentrated on the two shooters. The soldiers were behind rocks but were still partially visible. They could not fire at Ned without exposing themselves.

Above the din of the weapon fire, Ned heard the sound of another vehicle approaching. He looked over at the main path to the top of the hill and saw a vehicle that looked like a small troop carrier. As it quickly approached the wreckage, he could see probably eight to ten more soldiers, with two in the cab and the rest in the back. They had their weapons at the ready as the vehicle stopped, and they all jumped out, firing as they ran. Ned finished off the two behind the rocks and tried to position himself to defend against this new onslaught. His feelings of helplessness were never worse than right now.

He moved to a better vantage point that had better protection behind his shelter of rocks, but he was only able to bring the M16 and two and a half clips with him. He also had the .45 on his side holster with a fresh clip and one more in his pocket.

The enemy had spread out in about a fifty-yard range, making it difficult for Ned to concentrate his fire in one direction. He identified the ones he thought were closest to him and fired at them, with some success. Two enemy soldiers slumped to the ground as he sprayed their hiding place. He felt the burn of a bullet passing through his other shoulder, then another hit his helmet. He continued to fire single shoots, trying to make the bullets last, and he fortunately continued to find his targets.

This time, two soldiers were advancing on the rocks, firing as they came. He couldn't see their heads, but they had on flak jackets. He fired at their throats, hitting and immediately disabling both of them. It didn't seem to matter how many he hit, though. It felt like there were dozens of the enemy firing at him from every direction. He felt the sizzling burn of two bullets cutting into his back and side, so now he knew the enemy had reached the side of the shelter. He could no longer hide.

The toll from his new wounds and his earlier ones was too intense, and he could no longer stay awake. He felt himself slump and could not keep his eyes open. His brain and body began to shut down until he was totally unconscious.

As the Viet Cong soldiers overran Ned's shelter and found him sprawled on the ground, they heard the sound of a helicopter approaching. Rather than kill and leave him with the wreckage, two VC soldiers dragged him to one of the jeeps and pushed him into the back end. They sped into the jungle, hoping to avoid the firepower of the American helicopter.

The copter pilot saw the jeep speeding into the jungle but also saw several VC soldiers crawling around the wreckage and the rocks near it. The door gunner loaded up and blasted all six of them. The copter then turned toward the direction of the escaping jeep, but it was swallowed by the jungle. The copter returned to the wreckage and battlefield and landed close to the wreckage, where everyone but the pilot and door gunner jumped out to look for survivors.

There was also an intelligence officer aboard who would look for the satchel of classified material, as well as for the Intelligence officer who had been aboard the copter that was shot down. They found the bodies of the two pilots in the side of the rock formation. After more searching, they found the satchel stuck into the rocks and handed it to the Intelligence officer. He was relieved to find that the lock was still in place and the satchel undamaged. Unfortunately, their search for Ned was unsuccessful, and they could only assume that he had been captured.

11

Prisoner for Sale

[handwritten annotation: they said that we send]

THE TWO VIET CONG soldiers raced down the hill through the jungle, actually following the path that Ned had used to send the truck of dead Vietnamese down. As the Viet Cong reached the bottom of the hill and the bank of a rain swollen stream, they noticed a truck along the bank. It appeared to have crashed and burned, although it was partially submerged in the water.

They didn't notice any one in the truck, so they assumed they either walked away or were swept away by the current. It didn't matter to them either way because they were more interested in finding a boat that would carry them downstream to a North Vietnamese encampment. They had heard that it would be upstream from where this stream ran into the river.

They knew that an officer was worth a lot of money and other rewards to the North Vietnamese, so they were going to cash in with their prisoner. They just hoped he didn't die before they delivered him.

The swollen stream had washed a large amount of debris with its current, and among the tree limbs and other trash, they spotted a small boat that was stuck by a tree trunk on the bank only a few yards away from them.

They left Ned in the jeep and went down to loosen the boat from the tree trunk so they could then load Ned into it and float down the stream until it reached the river. They felt even luckier when they found that the boat had a small motor on it with almost a full tank of gas. That would make their trip even faster.

They grabbed some of the limbs that were holding up the tree trunk to use as guide poles to keep them from running aground as they guided the boat downstream. The motor would give them the speed, and they would keep it straight with the limbs.

They checked to see if Ned was still alive and, finding him actually breathing, loaded him into the bottom of the boat and headed down the stream, being cautious about who or what might be along the banks. The soldiers were very happy about their potential reward for bringing in an American officer. They even used some of their clothing to dry off the blood from his wounds. They didn't know if it would help, but they didn't know of anything else to do.

After several hours of following the swift current and then running out of gas, they could hear the sound of the rushing river water not far away. Their spirits lightened until they realized they wouldn't be able to travel upstream without gas or a bigger boat. But that was not going to slow them down. Watching both banks as they approached the river, they noticed what looked like an encampment on one of the stream's banks. They carefully surveyed the area for possible enemy soldiers. They decided to stop and possibly set up a camp themselves until they figured out how to get upstream.

12

Following Family Honor

Ben

FROM HIS YOUTH, Ben heard stories about the military and fighting in wars from his grandfather and dad. His grandfather Raymond had been in World War II, and his dad, Leroy, served in Korea. They were both engaged in trying to save American lives as medics rather than killing the enemy.

Raymond had been with the first Army troops to go to Africa, and after that, he moved on to Italy and more of the European war theater. He told of the heroics of many young men but also of the savagery of the war and severe wounds suffered by our troops. He would always end up in tears as he described trying to save lives and limbs, but he was often unsuccessful.

He was wounded several times, thankfully none of them severe but serious enough to eventually bring him home before the war was ended. He spent many months in Army hospitals and in rehabilitation centers before being released out of the Army and returned home. He would walk with a limp for the rest of his life, but he celebrated that he was alive.

Ben's father, Leroy, remembered his dad going into the Army right after Pearl Harbor. He was the oldest child and took his responsibility to care for his mother and siblings seriously. Leroy was sixteen when the family learned about his father's injuries, prompting him to quit school so that he could go to work. Leroy knew he would have to be the financial provider for his family, as well as their guardian, until his father was well enough to take back those responsibilities, assuming that he would someday be able to.

When Leroy was old enough—in his own opinion, of course—he married his high school sweetheart who was still in school, but they had her parents' permission to marry early. Ben and Gary's mother, Evana, were both seventeen when they married.

Raymond came home, and although he was disabled, he was able to find a good job with the railroad. Leroy was now able to venture out and be responsible for his own wife and soon-to-be children. Listening to his father's tales of the war, the service he was able to provide for the family, and the pride that he showed in what he had done, Leroy decided to join the Marines. Unfortunately for him, the Marines were being downsized, so he opted for the Army because they were always taking new enlistees. This was several years after the end of World War II and before the Korean Conflict became intense.

When he was struggling through basic training, he selected medic as his MOS, following in his father's footsteps. Also while he was in basic, he learned that he was going to be a father for the first time. He was happy and proud beyond belief, even more so when his baby son was born. They named him Ben because it was a good, strong name.

Toward the end of his first enlistment, as Korea was heating up, Leroy volunteered to go to South Korea and serve as a medic to the troops. He extended his enlistment for two years and then shipped off to Korea. His experience was unlike his father's as he served in the bitter cold fields, treating soldiers with frostbite and shrapnel wounds from the constant shelling from the North Koreans. Because he was a sergeant, his assignment was at a field hospital and not with the troops on the front lines or on the patrols in hostile areas. He saw and treated the worst of the wounds but was thankfully not subject to direct enemy fire, although a stray artillery shell would occasionally explode near the hospital.

He remained in Korea for eighteen months and then was sent back to the states and released from active duty early. Although he had not been wounded by enemy fire, Ben's father had emotional issues because of where he had been, what he had witnessed, and what he had to do. He would deal with these issues for many years, and it was the major cause of his divorce and inability to keep a job. Finally, he was hired by the post office, and he managed to keep that job for thirty years.

Ben knew that as he prepared to graduate from high school, he was destined to enter the military. Although he thought of many other professions he could go to and colleges that he could attend, he felt the military service was in his blood, and he needed to follow the family tradition of service to his country.

He decided that he was going to join the Navy and hopefully avoid the trauma of the battlefield that had permanently damaged his grandfather and father. He had a much better chance of serving aboard a ship or at some other duty station that was not in a war zone.

As he was progressing through Navy boot camp in Great Lakes, Illinois, Ben chose to make Hospital Corpsman his rate. He would follow in his family's footsteps but again figured that a Navy Corpsman would be a safe occupation. He was assigned to Corpsman school in San Diego, California, and performed very well. While in this school, he began hearing about the orders that the graduating classes ahead of him were receiving. Although many were assigned to ships or shore duty, the majority of the

Really?!

Corpsman graduates were being assigned to Marine units and, in most cases, were being sent to Vietnam. Everyone in the military knew that the Marines were always assigned to the toughest and most dangerous fronts in every war, and Vietnam was no exception. Ben tried to remain optimistic and thought that if he did well in his school, he would be assigned to a Naval unit rather than the Marines.

As graduation for his class approached, orders came down for them. Ben was grateful that he wasn't assigned to a Marine unit, but when he read his orders saying that he was assigned to a Seabee unit in Da Nang, South Vietnam, he was stunned and instantly frightened by the possibilities. Other than the Underwater Demolition Teams (UDT, Seals), the Seabees were the toughest Naval group and were known for their fighting capabilities as much as they were their construction accomplishments. They would be assigned to build roads, bridges, buildings—everything where there hadn't been anything before. This resulted in encountering the enemy on a regular basis and fighting while they were doing their construction work. It wasn't a Marine assignment, but it was the next worse thing that he could think of.

Ben struggled with his orders, and he thought, *I'm sure that my dad and grandfather were often afraid and feared for their lives, but they accepted their assignments and fulfilled their duties admirably. By the stories that they have told me, they did what they had to do bravely and without hesitation.*

I know that they want me to make the same commitment. I'm going to look forward to this challenge as an opportunity and live up to my family's legacy of service.

After completing Corpsman school and combat training, Ben spent two weeks at home prior to heading overseas.

While he was at home, his grandfather and father talked to Ben about serving in the war.

His dad said, "Ben, your grandfather and I are proud of you, and I know that you are going to be fine."

Ben felt proud and replied, "I want the two of you to be proud of me, and I'm going to be a great soldier just like you and Grandpa."

They were secretly afraid for him but would not let him see it.

His mother and siblings stayed as close to him as he would let them, wanting to get his attention and take advantage of the short time they had left with him. His friends had several going-away parties for him, and he probably drank more in those two weeks than he had ever done before.

The girl he dated in high school was around a lot, and they spent some quality time together and committed to write to each other every day while he was gone.

After a final family dinner and good conversations with his family, Ben went to the last scheduled going-away party. He drank more than usual, but his girlfriend took him to his house, where he passed out in his own bed. This would be his last night in that bed for a long time.

He was very groggy and hungover the next morning, but he managed to pack up his uniforms and other items he would be taking with him.

His parents and grandfather took him to the train station, expressed their love for each other, and Ben was off on his greatest challenge.

13

Construction in a War Zone

H IS TRAIN RIDE to Memphis, the flights to San
Francisco, and the bus to Travis AFB were uneventful.
At Travis, Ben reported to the Naval office and was told that
there were other members of his unit going to Da Nang,
and they needed to connect and stay together. He found
the eight Seabees awaiting the flight, and they spent the
next couple of hours getting acquainted. It was a mixture of
first-tour people, as well as several Seabees going back for
their second or third tour.

The experienced Seabees spoke the most, relating what
to expect when they got to their base. One of them said,
"There is enemy activity almost every day, either mortars,
artillery, or small patrols are sniping at them. There are
Marines assigned to the construction site, and they are
quick to repel any patrol, as well as call in artillery to wipe

out the mortar and artillery locations. It is dangerous, but the Marines believe in the work that they are doing, and they are willing to take the risk."

This was the most valuable information that Ben and the others had received. They began to feel more comfortable about their future assignment, although their fears were not eliminated.

They stayed together on their flight to Da Nang and continued the conversations. They were picked up at the airfield by the duty driver and taken to their base ten miles north, outside of the city. It was what they had expected, a series of Quonset huts and garages where vehicles were being repaired. The new arrivals were escorted to one of the Quonsets to meet the Commanding officer and Executive officer. After that, they were taken to their assigned barracks and told to make themselves at home. There was one other Corpsman among the new arrivals, so after getting their bunks and lockers in order, Ben and the other new Corpsman walked to the sick bay hut to meet the medical group. This would be their headquarters and where they would receive their assignments and other information.

Ben got settled in and began getting to know the other Corpsmen, the nurses, the doctors, the three nonmedical personnel who took care of records. He was assigned to one of the construction crews, where his job would be to accompany them on their projects and treat any injuries or illnesses. This would take him into the jungle but only for a few days at a time.

He began getting acquainted with the Seabees who he would be serving with, making friends with several of them. He developed a good friendship with an equipment operator named Johnny. They began hanging out together on their off days, drinking at the enlisted men's club, going to the movies when they were shown, and just hanging out. They both liked music and tried to play the guitar, so that was something else they had in common. Johnny's hometown was about two hundred miles from Ben's. They agreed they would get together when they got back to the world. It was good to have someone to hang out with and talk to. Everyone in Vietnam needed to share their thoughts and dreams and fears with someone. Ben and Johnny were equally good for each other, and that made their situation somewhat easier. Johnny had been with the unit for only two weeks before Ben arrived, so their time in country would be about the same. All things considered, they were both happy with the friendship and companionship.

Johnny was a heavy equipment operator, running bulldozers and other construction equipment. He often was clearing jungle paths where no American had ever been. It was high enough risk that there were Marines assigned to their unit to provide cover for the Seabees. There were several skirmishes with Viet Cong patrols, but the Marines quickly squashed them and kept the Seabees' mission moving forward.

After eight months, the construction project was progressing well, and their road was moving deeply into the jungle and would provide movement of equipment and troops and cutting off similar supply lines of the Viet Cong. As they moved deeper into the jungle, they encountered more enemy resistance.

The gun battles became more intense, and the mortar rounds were pounding their position. More Marines had to be assigned to provide security for the construction crews. This resulted in more Americans being wounded, some critically. Ben was very busy caring for the Marines and the Seabees, often keeping them alive until evacuation units could get in to fly them to field hospitals. Ben was earning his keep and was physically and emotionally exhausted when they were relieved by other units. Instead of movies and the club, he spent his off time sleeping, thinking of home and his girlfriend, regretting having to go back to the construction site, now a battlefield.

Johnny was fortunate that he had not been wounded or injured by the enemy attacks. The Seabees continued their mission of getting this road built in spite of the enemy and the rainy weather, the monsoon season.

14

TET Unceasefire

THERE WAS DISCUSSION of a ceasefire for the Tet holiday coming up. Ben, Johnny, and every other Seabee and Marine was sincerely hoping and praying that the rumor was true. Any break from the enemy's attacks and mortar bombardments would be very welcome. As the end of January approached, there was a sense of anticipation, hoping for a ceasefire but also the possibility of an increase in the enemy's activity. The North Vietnamese and Viet Cong couldn't be trusted and certainly were not predictable.

The last day of January clarified the possibilities. The enemy attacks began to intensify, and more troops were coming at the Americans than they had ever experienced. Trying to get one more day of construction done before they had to fall back to their base was not a good idea. The mortars came in hot and heavy, and their aim was truer than before. Equipment was being destroyed, and Seabees and Marines were falling wounded or dying everywhere on the work site. There were two other Corpsman with Ben this day, but all three were overwhelmed with the injuries. They tried to reach the most seriously wounded first to try to stop the bleeding and the cries of pain all around them.

The equipment operators who didn't have their machines blown out from under them abandoned the equipment and also tried to help the wounded. Ben spotted a Marine lying near the perimeter of the construction site and quickly crawled over to him. It was Dale, a young PFC who had taken hits to his shoulder blade, breaking bones, his thigh, and his head and knocking him unconscious. Bullets were now flying past him, but he had to do what he could for this fighter who had been his protector. Ben felt severe pain to the left side of his neck, momentarily jolting him to the ground and making him very dizzy. He tried to put a bandage on his wound but couldn't get it placed right. Another hand came in and grabbed the gauze and applied it to his neck wound. Ben looked up and recognized his friend Johnny kneeling next to him. Johnny was holding the bandage and kept firing with his .45 at anything that moved in the jungle. Ben regained most of his balance and wrapped more gauze around his own neck, which thankfully only had a glancing wound, although it was bleeding like crazy. He tied it off tightly and went back to treating Dale.

Johnny picked up the Marine's M16 and began firing bursts into the jungle where he thought he had seen rifle fire. He didn't know if he was hitting anyone, but he knew he had to keep trying to protect his friend who was saving a Marine.

As Ben continued his tasks, he saw Johnny fall back onto the ground; he had been hit in the shoulder. Then he took another hit, this time to his leg, possibly cracking his kneecap. Johnny was now in great pain and was no longer able to fire his weapons. Ben grabbed more bandages and crawled to Johnny. He felt another bullet hit the back of his helmet, right on the red cross. He was again stunned but continued crawling to his friend.

He looked around and saw the massacre of his group. The Marines and Seabees were falling everywhere; he also saw the other two Corpsman prostrate on the ground, not moving and not making a sound. He assumed the worst. As he tried to move from Johnny to Dale, the sound of weapons grew quieter, although he could still hear the ugly sound of mortars being launched. He was still dizzy and unable to truly focus, but he knew he held two lives in his hand and had to do whatever he could to keep them alive. He did not notice the six Viet Cong soldiers approaching him and his wounded. Suddenly he felt the barrel of a rifle poke him in the back of his neck. He froze, waiting for the weapon to fire, saying what he knew would be his last prayer.

Instead, he heard the Viet Cong soldier yelling at him and motioning him to get up. Ben didn't get up because he had to finish the bandages on Johnny's knee and shoulder. The enemy soldier poked him again, this time harder, and yelled even louder, clicking back the chamber like he was going to shoot this time. Ben finished the wrap, then stood up slowly, still very light-headed from the hit to his head and the bleeding from his neck. As he got to his feet, the Viet Cong hit him across his face with the butt of his rifle, knocking him to the ground, making him even more light-headed and hurting with a freshly broken and bleeding nose. He drifted in and out of consciousness, but he was aware of what was happening, at least to a limited degree.

The six enemy soldiers grabbed Dale, Johnny, and Ben under their arms and dragged them back into the jungle. American prisoners would be very valuable to the North Vietnamese Army that was only twenty-five kilometers away. The enemy soldiers took then back to an old truck, loaded them into the back, and took off toward the river.

They would take them to a holding area along the river and keep them there until they contacted the North Vietnamese. They would turn the Americans over to them for whatever they wanted to do with them. They didn't care as long as they were rewarded for delivering the hated Americans.

15

Viet Cong Scum

A S THEY DROVE off with their captives, the rest of the Viet Cong troops took all the weapons and supplies that they could carry. They didn't intend to take any more prisoners, so any American who was still moving or breathing was shot and killed. They also placed grenades under and in all the construction equipment to make sure that the Americans could not use it again. After collecting their spoils, the Viet Cong disappeared back into the jungle, proud to have delivered a damaging defeat to the hated Americans.

The six Viet Cong with the American captives drove the short distance to the river, where they had hidden a large boat with a good motor that was stolen from some South Vietnamese fishermen. They dragged the Americans into the boat, and four of them took off upstream, where they had built a small encampment along the banks of a large stream that ran into the river. The other two returned with the truck to their unit and excitedly told their comrades what they had done.

When they arrived at their encampment, the four Viet Cong pulled the Americans ashore and rested briefly, relishing their accomplishment. They were going to be rich and hopefully would be able to go home and not have to fight anymore. They pulled their boat up into the brush so that it couldn't be spotted from the stream or the river.

As they caught their breath and bragged to one another, they heard voices that sounded like they were coming from down the stream. They quickly grabbed their weapons and watched for the boat approaching their camp. They saw the boat approaching and then saw it come ashore by their hidden boat. They recognized the occupants as fellow Viet Cong soldiers and yelled out to welcome them.

The six enemy soldiers met at the center of the encampment and introduced themselves. They exchanged stories and realized they were doing the same thing for the same reasons. The soldiers congratulated each other and allowed the stories about their own bravery and heroics to grow substantially. They discussed how to get their prisoners to the North Vietnamese Army and how they would split the booty. One of them was more senior with the Viet Cong and was also the oldest, so he was given command of their straggly group. He asked for ideas on how to hold the Americans until they were ready to transport them upstream. The decision was made to put them in the water with their hands and feet bound, deep enough to keep only their heads above water. They wanted to humiliate and torture the Americans in any way they could without killing them. There was a place in the river where the current wasn't swift, and it was close to the encampment, so they could watch them while enjoying the comfort of a fire and food. They only wish they had some rice wine to make it even better. They dragged the four Americans on shore, and it was clear that the American officer was in the worst condition, and another one of the others was also seriously wounded. The other two were not as badly injured. The Viet Cong soldiers tied a healthier one to a seriously injured one, which would keep the healthier ones from escaping and hopefully keep the more seriously wounded from drowning.

There was a lot of money to be made from these prisoners if they were alive. They had no medical supplies and wouldn't know what to do with them if they did, so they decided to just put all four Americans into the water and hope for the best.

They next needed a plan for their trip and the supplies they would need. They would definitely need a lot more gas to fight the river's swift current going upstream. They also needed more food and maybe even some fresher clothes since most of theirs were bloody and muddy from the stream's bank.

They decided to eat what supplies they had, and then four of them would head upstream to look for a village. It had taken them most of the day to make their plan. It would be getting dark soon, so they would be able to steal what they needed from the village inhabitants. The villagers would be too frightened to challenge them, fearing they would be killed.

The Viet Cong ate their meal, and then two of them took the leftovers, with some added river water, to their prisoners. Not surprisingly, none of them ate anything. As it grew dark, it was time for the four to leave for their mission of theft. The two youngest members would stay behind and take turns on watch. It was a good plan, and everyone again congratulated each other.

The four departed and headed their boat upstream, hopeful of finding a helpless village to steal their supplies.

A few kilometers away, they saw some fires burning, and as they got closer, they saw about ten huts that had been built about fifty meters from the riverbank. There was a dock that had several fishing boats attached, so they quickly went through them looking for fuel. They found several full tanks and ran them back to their own boat. They then went into the village and knocked in doors, demanding food and clothing. The poor villagers were not going to resist or deny them whatever they wanted. They were given more food than they could eat in a week, many articles of clothing that were old but useable, and a large supply of rice wine. Not surprisingly, the mission became less urgent as they decided to enjoy some of the wine before heading back.

After consuming several bottles, they decided there should be more entertainment, so they made the villagers come out and sing for them. There were also several attractive girls in the village, so the drunken Viet Cong soldiers forced the young girls to have sex with them right in plain sight of their families. The soldiers only laughed and continued to drink.

Finally, only one of them was still awake, so he shook the others awake and made them get back on their boat. They had already loaded everything, so they pushed off with the most sober one running the motor and guiding the boat back downstream.

The others again passed out, and soon, even the sober one had to give in to his intoxication and started falling asleep. He was cognizant enough to land the boat on shore before totally passing out.

They remained on the bank for several hours until the sun started relighting the day. One by one, they awoke and poked the others until they were all groggily awake. The older soldier started the motor and headed the boat back to the encampment, feeling very sick but satisfied with their night's work. The sun was just peeking above the mountains when they made the turn into the stream and toward their camp.

16

The Only Choice

TOM DECIDED IT would be a good time to pull the tree trunk to shore and check the surroundings for activity, and possibly find some food he could catch or kill. The bulk of the trunk made it difficult to get to shore, but he finally managed to find a slow spot in the current along one bank, and then he tied the ends of the trunk to trees along the shore.

Assured that his ride would be here when he returned, he climbed the steep bank and began observing the surrounding areas, looking on both sides of the stream. He was especially curious about the loud water noises and headed in the direction of the rushing waters.

As he cautiously advanced, he heard noises that sent shivers up and down his spine. He faintly heard laughter and then voices that were not speaking English. He had heard enough Vietnamese to know that these people were speaking one of the many Vietnamese dialects. Although one or two of the voices were high pitched, Tom surmised they were likely all men, soldiers of either the North or the South because both could be in this area.

His first instinct was to either turn and run back to the tree trunk or to stay where he was and hoped they weren't patrolling in his direction, but his curiosity, and maybe his soldier mentality, took control, and he carefully advanced toward the voices to properly evaluate their origin.

The jungle was thick enough, the terrain rolling enough, and the noise of the rushing water loud enough that Tom thought he could approach the source of the voices carefully but undetected. As the voices became more distinct, Tom began to crawl toward them, being as silent as possible and not disturbing more brush than needed. He reached the crest of a small rise in the jungle, and he could see a small encampment next to the stream he had been floating on. If he had not stopped when he did, he would have floated right past them, and who knows what may have happened. God was working on his side. At least he hoped he was.

He was able to raise up enough to survey the encampment, and to his disbelief, he saw four men positioned in the water. They were sitting back to back in about three feet of water, barely keeping their heads from being submerged. They appeared very weak, but he noticed that they were helping each other, preventing the man next to them from slipping into the water.

He could see them well enough to recognize the cuts, scratches, and bruises on their heads and faces, so he could only imagine how their bodies must look. He felt at once sickened and boiling mad, but also very afraid. He knew he had to keep his emotions under control because if he acted without a plan, it would likely result in his own death or capture, as well as possibly further endangering the Americans being held captive.

Tom couldn't believe this was happening to him. He wasn't a real soldier, wasn't brave or in any way prepared to know what to do.

He sat there quietly and thought, *I feel like running away on my own down the river to the safety of the American outpost, but I couldn't live with myself if I didn't try to help these American soldiers who are in danger. I hate this. Why am I here, and why do these men's lives have to be in my hands? If I run away, no one will know but me. I would have to live with that the rest of my life. If I try to rescue them, I'm probably going to get killed or captured and tortured like them. My God, how can I do this? I can't run, so I have to think about what a real warrior would do and how I can rescue these men. I must develop a plan that will ensure the safety of those men and my own skin. I don't want to do this, but it can't be done without me. Dammit!*

Tom's mind began working on not just a plan to rescue them but also an escape plan that will take them all to safety.

He began to observe the activities of the Viet Cong soldiers, mentally tracking their movements, their storage areas, and the location of their weapons, as well as the numbers and ammo for them. He saw them bringing items from their boat and the distance they walked to and from the boat. He tried very hard to note everything they were doing and the length of time needed for each activity.

As hours passed, Tom began to feel acquainted with the activities and with each guard's habits. They all smoked, one laughed incessantly, and another seemed to be giving orders and directing the activities of the other five. As shabby as they looked, they acted like they knew what they were doing. He surmised that this was a temporary holding area for the Americans until they would be picked up and taken to a camp or other holding area—or until they died.

The stories were always being told about Americans who disappeared or were captured, then tortured and humiliated until they died. Their bodies would be disposed of and never found, only their dog tags.

Time was at once standing still and racing forward in Tom's mind. He wanted to rescue the Americans and kill the enemy soldiers, but he still didn't know how to do it. He also had to pick the right time that would bring the best opportunity to successfully save them and destroy the evil ones. He had to bide his time for the right chance. He believed he was not the right man for the job, but there were no other options.

17

Breathe Deep, Do the Deed

*T*HIS IS IT, he thought to himself. The darkness surrounding him made the guard close to the fire look even brighter and larger. The other four Viet Cong would hopefully be gone long enough for Tom to execute his plan. He crawled and then walked around the encampment to stay in the thickest jungle brush. He was about eight feet from the Viet Cong soldier and stopped to make one more assessment of his plan.

Tom believed that he was close enough now to rush up behind the enemy soldier and slit his throat before he could make a sound. Hopefully the other soldier would remain sleeping, making Tom's second kill even easier. He took another deep breath, wiped the tears from his eyes, felt the handle of the knife in his sweaty and shaking hand, thought, *This is it, Lord*, and jumped into the open space between himself and the guard.

The guard was stooped close to the fire and didn't appear to even notice Tom until he grabbed him around the head to muffle his mouth, causing the enemy to spring up into Tom's grasp. Tom raised the knife and ran it across the soldier's neck, but it didn't do anything; Tom had the blade turned backward! He quickly turned the knife around in his hand, cursed his stupidity, and tried again as the enemy struggled in his arm to get free, showing remarkable strength. But Tom's grasp was even stronger as he quickly pressed the blade against the small neck, severing all the nerves, airways, and everything else that would instantly silence the Cong and lead to his almost immediate death.

Tom dropped him to the ground and ran to the sleeping soldier, who seemed to be raising up in a daze but staring at the fire and not at Tom. Tom acted quickly, grabbing the sleepy enemy by the head and slicing his neck in one swift movement. He had no doubt they were both dead as massive pools of blood surrounded both of them. Tom's hands, arms, and shirt were also covered in the warm thickening red blood of the two enemy soldiers, no longer a threat to anyone.

He could not believe what he had done. He was shaking profusely, his eyes filling with tears, and he almost fell down because his knees were so weak, but he knew that he had to press on to complete his plan and what was now his mission.

With his knife still in his hand, Tom ran into the water and began cutting the ropes and dragging the Americans from the water as quickly as he could. He pulled all four out and laid them close to the heat of the fire, then started checking their condition. Two of them responded and seemed partially coherent. One was unconscious but was slowly showing some response, but the fourth man appeared very badly wounded and needing the most attention. Tom wasn't a medic, but he knew that he had to get them into dry clothing or get their clothing dry as quickly as possible. He pulled the clothes off of the two dead Viet Cong. Even though the clothing was bloody, it was still drier than the Americans'.

He threw the clothes at the two conscious Americans, and they undressed. He grabbed the bedding that the sleeping enemy had been using and draped it over the unconscious American. He opened the other Viet Cong's pack and pulled out his bedding for the second badly wounded American. He ran back to his pack and brought it back to use all the spare clothing and anything else to cover the seriously wounded men.

There was enough to at least cover them, and he hoped the warmth of the fire would help the men find new life. Getting them all warmed and closer to dry was the main priority. Tom had no medical treatment to offer, only the covers and the fire. As the two strongest men started to revive, he offered them the rations he had, as well as the water he had left in his canteen. He now had to figure out their next step.

He took the time to introduce himself, and they told Tom who they were and where they had been captured. They did not know the story of the Naval Officer because he had been brought by two different Viet Cong than who had captured them and Dale, the unconscious Marine.

He wasn't certain when the other Viet Cong soldiers would return, but he guessed there was about three hours until day break. Although his priority was keeping the Americans alive and regaining some strength, he knew he must plan for the enemies' return and how they would handle it. He not only needed to kill the four who that returned, but he also needed their boat in hopes of taking the men to the safety of an American outpost.

He brought all his supplies to the campsite and used everything he had to try to comfort the American soldiers.

While looking at the three Americans, he thought, *These men are the real heroes. They have suffered at the hands of ruthless and merciless enemies, receiving treatment that would eventually lead to their deaths. No person deserves this treatment, even if they are at war.*

His mind briefly took him to acting in revenge, making these other four Vietnamese suffer like they had made the Americans suffer, but he knew they didn't have time, and that wasn't what Americans did. He grew angrier and more intent than he thought he could possibly be.

He heard the man closest to death moan and move slightly, forcing Tom to refocus on the task at hand to save these men as soon as possible. The two stronger men began moving about and were checking on the other two.

Tom asked, "Do you think that you will be able to help me when the enemy soldiers return?"

Ben and Johnny said, "We are more than ready to help kill those little bastards!"

Tom was gratified by their resolve but knew they would be limited by their weakness. He again admired their bravery. They began to develop a plan that would involve the three of them, with Ben and Johnny at least being able to fire a weapon when the time was right.

He took the bodies of the two dead Viet Cong and put some of the shredded clothing from the Americans on them and set their bodies in the water where the captives had been. He strapped them down back to back so they would not float or drift away with the current. They wouldn't look like Americans in the daylight, but if the boat returned before it was bright enough, they likely would not notice the difference. He only had two bodies to replace the four Americans, but he hoped that they would think the other two had died and either sunk or floated downriver, so only two remained.

He had to take that risk because he didn't see other choices other than putting the Americans back in the water, and he wasn't going to do that. He then took branches of burning wood from the fire and started a second fire in the thick jungle, where it wouldn't be easy to detect from the river or the creek. He built the fire as big as he thought would be safe, then with Ben and Johnny's help, dragged the two most seriously wounded Americans to the new fire area. He knew had to keep them warm and dry, even if there was no way to treat their wounds. Tom watched as Ben began treating the two seriously wounded men with the meager clothes and other items he found in Tom's supplies.

That is the best blessing of all, Tom thought. *He's a medic*! Tom noticed that both of them were moving more and breathing more easily. He allowed a wave of optimism to pass through his brain. Maybe all five of them could survive!

The weapons that the two dead Viet Cong had would now be used by the strongest American soldiers. He positioned them far enough into the jungle that they were not visible but had clear vision of the campsite. He instructed them to not fire until he fired the first rounds, then they were to open up and shoot the closest Viet Cong to them, making sure to hit at least one of them immediately. Both Americans acted excited about the opportunity to kill their former captors, but Tom reminded them how important it was to wait until they heard him fire.

The thought came into Tom's head, *Here is the whiner. The cowardly one was actually directing real warriors.* He could not believe he had it in himself.

He positioned himself close to the water where the boat would land, likewise hidden but able to see the enemies' activities. As he tucked himself into the brush, night began giving way to the dull light of dawn. This was the first time Tom had stopped all night, and he suddenly realized how tired he was. It had been an extremely eventful night, and his body was not used to the rigors he had put it through.

He still couldn't believe that he hadn't run away and had actually killed two people. He would never expect his former fellow soldiers to believe what he had done because he almost couldn't believe it himself. Adrenaline was still rushing through his body, and he stayed focused on what was about to happen.

His plan was to wait until the Viet Cong soldiers had landed and secured the boat and were headed toward the campsite. As they neared the campsite, he would move out to be behind them, and when the best opportunity presented itself, he would shoot the closest Viet Cong to him and keep firing until all four went down or somehow managed to hide from his sight. He hoped between his shots and the other two Americans, they would take out all four of the enemy soldiers and not have to deal with a battery of shots coming at them.

It was a simplistic plan, but it was the best he could come up with. It would work if all when right. This wasn't Tom's strength, planning and instructing others, and he wasn't very good at hard work, but now he had managed to be better than even he thought possible.

18

Fight to Live, On to Freedom

A BOVE THE ROAR of the river, he faintly heard the sound of a motorboat; Tom's skin tingled, and he felt the hair on the back of his neck stiffen. *This was it*, he thought. *Kill or be killed.*

He was afraid and regretted what he had to do, but he knew they had to do it to save the Americans and himself. Their only hope was at once extremely frightening and exhilarating. Tom's feelings were very difficult to explain, or even understand, but it was a rush like he had never experienced.

The sound of the boat's motor grew louder and Tom knew he had to be most watchful right now. He couldn't allow the enemy to see him or anything out of place at the campsite as they approached.

The boat came into Tom's sight as it turned into the creek from the river. He could now see there were four soldiers and several containers of what were likely supplies. As they grew closer, he could even hear discussions taking place. One soldier was in the front of the boat and began to untether a rope that he would use to pull the boat ashore and secure it to a tree or other object. The soldier in the rear of the boat was steering and operating the motor, slowing down as they approached the shore. So far, all was going as Tom had hoped and planned. As the boat reached the shore, the front soldier jumped out and pulled the boat up onto the beach. He tied the rope to a nearby tree to make sure it didn't get pulled away by the swift current of the stream.

The other three enemy soldiers began disembarking from the boat after the rear soldier had turned off the motor and raised the prop. The apparent leader of the squad then yelled toward the campsite, likely calling the two guards who had been there overnight. When there was no response, he yelled again. This time, it seemed he called out two names. Again not receiving a response, the four began talking with the motor operating soldier still in the boat. They grabbed their weapons, and the last one remained on the boat.

This was not the way Tom had envisioned this going down. The three soldiers began walking up the hill toward the campsite, continuing to yell out for the other soldiers. The boat-guarding soldier was now standing at the ready with his weapon in hand, scanning the entire area of the shore for movement.

The three enemy soldiers approached the campsite and saw no activity and no acknowledgement from the two night guards. They also noticed that there were only two people in the water instead of the four that had been there when they left. After reaching the opening to the campsite, the lead soldier noticed the signs of people moving around the camp. He saw the large pools of what looked like dried blood on the ground. He yelled at the other two, apparently telling them to return to the boat. Tom knew that he had to act now.

From his camouflaged position, Tom took aim and shot the soldier in the boat. He moved out from the brush and began firing at the remaining three. He heard shots coming from the jungle, and two of the enemy fell, leaving just the one leader. Tom fired repeatedly, and the enemy returned fire until he fell. Tom felt a sharp burning sensation in his chest and another on the side of his head. He knew he was hit, but he knew he couldn't stop now. He walked up to the body of the lead soldier and fired a shot into his head, not wanting to take any chances that he was still alive.

Tom walked over to the other two enemy soldiers and again shot them in the head until his clip was empty. As he finished, the two American soldiers came out of the jungle, jubilant that they had each shot one of the enemy. The three Americans met in the campsite and congratulated each other. It was then that the pain in Tom's chest manifested itself. He had been hit in the right side between his shoulder and sternum, likely shattering a rib or two and possibly hitting his lung. Tom sat there in pain, and while looking at his body, he thought, *At least the wounds are not on the left or middle. I think that I got very lucky.*

He also noticed large amount of blood on the right side of his head. It didn't really hurt, but the enemy's shot had obviously hit a bleeder. Tom used his hand to feel it, and the wound was gushing heavily. Ben grabbed Tom's socks from his pack and applied it to his head wound. Surprisingly the chest wound wasn't really bleeding in the front or back where it exited. Tom began feeling woozy but knew their work wasn't done.

He asked Ben and Johnny, "Do you think that you are strong enough to bring the other two American soldiers from the jungle down to the boat? I don't think I can do much."

They eagerly agreed, "You bet!"

Tom could sense that their excitement of getting free overcame their lack of strength. Tom staggered toward the boat and untied the rope from the tree. He was feeling light-headed and dizzy, but he had to fight through it because he had a job to finish. He finished untying the rope while Ben and Johnny were dragging Ned and Dale down the embankment to the boat. Ben and Johnny loaded the weaker Ned and Dale onto the boat and laid them on the bundles of supplies that were still in it.

Tom asked Ben and Johnny, "Do either of you know how to run a motorboat?"

Johnny replied, "I can. I used to have a fishing boat back home."

Tom said, "Thanks, man. I need you to guide the boat back to the river and head downstream as fast as you can."

He attempted to push the boat off of the shore but had to have Ben help because he was becoming noticeably weaker. They managed to push off, and Johnny pulled it away from shore and guided it to the river, then headed downstream as Tom had directed. The current was swift and helped the boat go much faster than it would have been capable of on its own. They didn't know what lay ahead, but they were going in what they believed was the direction of freedom.

Tom's chest began to hurt more as they moved swiftly down the river. It still wasn't bleeding, so he thought must mean he was bleeding on the inside. His head began to throb, but the pressure from holding the sock on his wound made the bleeding slow significantly.

His chest kept increasing in pain, and he felt like it was expanding from the inside. Tom began to drift out of consciousness. He fought it as long as he could because he had to be a help to his fellow Americans. Soon he couldn't keep his eyes or mind opened, and he lost consciousness completely.

Ben was trying to care for all three of the injured Americans, grabbing some of the clean clothing from the boat and tried to clean everyone's wounds. Unfortunately, since Tom's wound was bleeding internally, there wasn't much he could do.

He covered Tom with whatever clothing he could find and pulled him into the hull of the boat so he would hopefully stay drier. Ben hoped that Tom would be able to hold on until they reached an American unit.

Tom drifted in and out of consciousness, raising up to look at the surroundings as the boat sped down the river. Johnny was keeping it in the middle of the river, and everyone was staying as low in the boat just in case enemy soldiers along the shore recognized them as non-Vietnamese and opened fire.

Tom would attempt to get up, but he couldn't breathe when he raised up to a sitting position, so he would have to lay back down. He would soon give in to unconsciousness in spite of his best efforts to stay awake. After several ins and outs, Tom slipped into a total unconscious state and did not awaken again on the boat.

19

Rescued but May Be Dead

*W*HAT IS HAPPENING? Tom thought. He could see a group of people who appeared to be doctors and nurses working on him. One was performing CPR on his chest, another placing an oxygen mask over his mouth and nose, and others seeming to do different things. He even saw himself lying on an examination table, looking like he was dead.

He watched for several seconds as the medical team worked hard to revive him and admired their efforts. It didn't last long as their efforts brought him back, but he was still in a coma.

What seemed like only minutes later, it happened again. Tom was watching the medical team rushing around and doing whatever they could to get his heart working again. They had tubes inserted into his lungs to drain the excess blood that had filled one side. They had other IVs in his arms and his legs, feeding whatever medications he needed into his system. He could only continue admiring their efforts.

He actually wanted to tell them to stop because his mind told him that he was very happy and comfortable where he was. It was a feeling of freedom and painlessness and total happiness. These were amazing feelings that he knew he couldn't experience in his human lifetime. Soon their efforts worked, and he again became comatose, making these wonderful feelings only a very faint memory.

The boat had continued down the river as the two conscious Americans, Ben and Johnny, kept watching for some sign of an American boat or outpost. They saw several boats with Vietnamese fisherman, thankfully not Viet Cong soldiers. They didn't encounter any enemy resistance or come under attack from enemy soldiers on the river banks.

Finally, they spotted a boat coming up the river at a relatively high rate of speed. To their great relief, it was a US Navy patrol boat flying the American flag! They waved and yelled and steered the small boat toward the American boat. The patrol boat immediately approached them and boarded the five Americans into their boat and headed back South to their base.

Ben and Johnny collapsed when they were pulled onto the American boat, and both sobbed uncontrollably. Only hours before, they would have likely faced a torturous existence until they would eventually die at the hands of a hateful and heartless enemy. Now they were in American hands, heading to proper medical care and life, life that they didn't know would ever happen again. They didn't hide their feelings or their gratitude. They owed Tom their lives, and they wanted to express their thankfulness, but he needed immediate medical attention. They prayed openly for his survival and positive recovery. They would be eternally grateful. Even as they rejoiced, cried, and prayed, exhaustion overcame them, and they passed out.

Dale and Ned were receiving the best care from the Corpsman aboard the boat, and they were the first off the boat when they arrived at the boat's base. They had suffered gunshot wounds that had not been treated and had both developed pneumonia. Ned had more critical injuries and received the most attention from the Corpsman. The Captain of the boat radioed ahead for medical assistance for all five of the rescued American and informed the hospital of the conditions of each of them. He emphasized the importance of these men's lives and what they had already been through. The Captain told the base that even though all lives are important, these five men deserved the best.

Tom died several times in the field hospital, but each time, the medical team was able to revive him. They noticed he had an unusual faint smile on his face that even the doctors couldn't explain. Tom had only a faint memory of his dying experiences, but there was a strange feeling of comfort that he could not explain.

The doctors and medical staff took his recovery very seriously and refused to let him die (or stay dead). They didn't know his story, but they knew he was someone who had done something very special and deserved their best efforts. They were thankful that Tom was a young healthy fighter whose body wasn't ready to let go.

Tom's wounds were potentially fatal if he hadn't received treatment when he did. His head wound was deep and took part of his skull bone, causing a severe concussion. As serious as the head wound was, the chest wound was even worse.

The bullet had broken a rib that was driven back into his right lung, puncturing it and causing the lung to collapse and bleed inside Tom's chest. The blood had no outlet because it wasn't near the bullet's entry or exit points, so it ran into his chest cavity, putting pressure on his heart and other internal organs. He lost multiple units of blood, and his entire system began to shut down because of the lack of blood flow.

His death was not unexpected, but somehow, the medical staff that saw all the worst of battle injuries fought for and achieved a remarkable life-saving effort.

Tom didn't know what was happening to him. When he wasn't dying, he remained unconscious and clearly comatose. He remained alive but not knowing anything for several weeks. This state kept him from feeling most of the pain that his body was experiencing as it was fighting the injuries and infections and starting to heal.

He was given massive doses of antibiotics, and the doctors didn't attempt to revive him from the coma. The pain he would have felt if he was conscious would have been unbearable, and his mind would have actually fought the healing because his feelings would have changed the healing focus that his body was imposing on itself.

Tom was transferred to a hospital ship after receiving the immediate vital care in Da Nang. He remained on the ship for several days until his condition began to stabilize. He was then airlifted to the Army hospital in Japan.

His vital signs improved, and the examinations of his wounds revealed continuing recovery. The doctors gradually reduced the level of pain medication Tom was receiving and planned for his return to consciousness. They were still concerned about his pain level but believed he was strong enough to fight it physically and emotionally on his own, although some level of pain medication would still be needed.

20

Awakening and Recoveries

Tom's mind slowly began to generate cognitive thoughts. He didn't open his eyes or even move, but his mind began to function and bring memories and thoughts into his head. His images became clearer and understandable. As his brain came into better focus, he began to also feel his body informing him that he was experiencing pain and discomfort. He attempted to move and try to relieve the hurt and began to feel his appendages and their aching because of inactivity.

He tried moving his legs slightly, and they responded by shakenly moving slowly, but moving ever so slightly. Without opening his eyes, he tried moving his arms, hands, and fingers, being cautious because he didn't want to hurt worse.

Tom was very stiff, but everything was moving at his will. *Am I ready to open eyes and see if I'm still alive?*

He began to notice noise around him, mumbled voices and body movements that he couldn't comprehend but was conscious of them nonetheless. He decided he should try opening his eyes to see if they would also work. They fluttered and fought him, but he finally got his left eye to open slightly. He tried to focus but had to close it after a short trial. Both eyes fluttered again, then he tried to open them. This time, the left opened, and the right followed ever so slowly and slightly. His mind was picking up the sounds better now and was receiving the visions from his eyes opening.

He felt a warm wet cloth wiping his eyes, and his vision became clearer. The blurry vision of a beautiful angel dressed in white and smiling brightly appeared. He thought he really had died, and he was thankful that he was in heaven!! He heard the angel speaking to him, and the angel in white became an Army nurse, still beautiful and still smiling but now talking to him. It took Tom a while to understand what she was saying to him.

"Welcome back to the land of the living, soldier," the nurse with beautiful smile greeted him. "You've been through a lot, but it is great that you're awake and all of your appendages are working. I'm sure your arms and legs are slow and stiff, but we will get them loosened up, and you'll be as good as new."

Tom felt himself smiling slightly and then trying to speak words that weren't ready to form. The smiling nurse reassured him, "Don't worry about speaking yet. You need to take your time and let all of your senses and functions work properly."

He was feeling happy but couldn't stay awake. Sleep now took the place of the comatose state.

Tom took his time and the healing process began. His recovery was quicker than the doctors expected, and he was attempting to walk within days of his return to consciousness. He continued to progress physically and mentally. The nurses filled in the course of events that occurred after he lost consciousness.

The four Americans he rescued were treated at the Navy's medical unit and then shipped via helicopter to the same hospital ship as Tom. Ned, the Naval officer who was in the worst condition, was still recovering in the Naval hospital in Hawaii. He was expected to recover, although it was too early to know the prognosis of his long-term condition. Ned had to have a kidney removed because of a severe infection. He had lost so much blood before they were rescued that he was fighting severe blood poisoning. It would be many months of recovery and rehabilitation to make him feel like a man again.

The next seriously wounded, the Marine, Dale, was shipped to the Naval hospital in Naha, Okinawa, and released after a few weeks to a rehabilitation hospital in the States. The shattered shoulder blade he suffered would limit his range of motion and movement of his left upper body. The other two less seriously wounded, a Navy Seabee named Johnny and Ben, a Navy Corpsman, were shipped to a Naval hospital in Japan.

Johnny's fractured knee kept him on crutches for several months, but he was progressing well. Ben would recover ahead of the rest, but he would still need some rehab on his shoulder. Their war zone as assignments were over, and they would soon be civilians.

They had all survived.

21

Back in the World, but It's Not Home

Tom was recognized by the Army with the Silver Star, along with two Purple Hearts and a Bronze Star. He was assigned to rehabilitation in Hawaii, then back to the States for his next duty. His heroics were never publicized because of the state of the American press and the political climate.

Even though their heroic duty wasn't going to be publicly recognized, the four Americans were thankful to be given back their lives. They would be eternally grateful for Tom's willingness to risk his life to save theirs.

After Ned was released from the hospital, he was assigned to a VA rehabilitation center near his hometown. He endured constant pain from his injuries. He had lost a substantial amount of his memory and cognitive thinking because of the head wounds he had suffered. Ned was miserable and felt that he was never going to get well and that he would always be a burden to his family.

After one of his appointments at the VA hospital, he received a refill of his painkillers. Ned went to his room, wrote a good-bye letter to his parents, and then swallowed the contents of his painkiller pill bottle. He went to sleep and did not wake up. He survived less than a year after returning from war.

Ned's family was devastated at his death. They were extremely proud of him because he had protected the bodies of the two pilots. They could only imagine how heartbreaking it would have been if the pilots were never recovered. His family was never made aware of the contents of the satchel that he had protected and the positive information it contained for the military leadership in Vietnam or of the severe negative impact it would have had on our troops if the information had been lost to and compromised to the enemy.

Ned was quietly buried in Arlington National cemetery, next to other American heroes. Ned was awarded the Silver Star, the Navy Cross, the Purple Heart with clusters, three Bronze Stars, and other heroism awards that the military could give him. Ned was not awarded the Medal of Honor. The Secretary of the Navy recommended it, but the Secretary of Defense wouldn't forward it to the President. The Secretary of Defense was afraid that presenting the highest honor to someone who had killed so many of the enemy might further damage the political status of the President. It was a thankless war, and Ned was one of the unthanked thousands.

Dale recovered enough from his injuries to be assigned as a Marine Recruiter near his hometown, even with his permanent disabilities, which limited his physical abilities. The war was still very vivid in his mind, and he was continuously seeking to bury his memories or attempting to drink them away. He woke up almost nightly sweating profusely and yelling unintelligible screams.

He met a woman in a bar, and they dated for a few months before making a trip to Las Vegas and getting married. They had two children, even though the woman recognized her Marine had serious issues. Dale had a serious drinking problem but was not willing to do anything about it. Eventually she left him and took the children with her.

This gave Dale an excuse to drink even more. He was going home from the bar one clear but chilly night, thinking about a similar night when he was submerged to his neck in a river, wondering how long he had to live. His mind focused on his memories, consuming his thoughts worse than ever, bringing back the fear and the pain he had experienced, feelings of not being worthy to even still be alive. He lost all touch with reality for minutes, and he was totally diverted from his driving and direction. His mind began to clear, but it was too late. By then, he had veered off the roadway at a very high rate of speed, crashing through brush and dropping down a deeply inclined ditch, running head-on into a tree. He was killed instantly.

Dale had received medals for his bravery and wartime experiences, but he was never able to filter the memories from controlling his life. He received a funeral with full military honors and burial in his State's Veteran's cemetery.

His former wife and children were there and were pleased with the recognition Dale received, thinking about how great of a husband and father he could have been to them if he hadn't had the serious issues after serving in Vietnam.

Johnny got out of the Navy and continued his heavy equipment operating vocation. He traveled around the country for different construction projects, advancing to a contracting manager for a large national company.

He never settled in one place because he was always restless and antsy. Johnny had mental and physical health issues, and he was smart enough to seek help. He spent many years in counseling and attending AA meetings. The help that he was receiving allowed him to maintain life again and worked well enough to keep Johnny close to balanced.

At the age of forty-five, Johnny was diagnosed with liver and pancreatic cancer, which the doctors believed was related to the chemicals he had been exposed to in the military, specifically Agent Orange.

Johnny fought the incurable cancer and lived until he was forty-eight. His work history was exceptional and known to many. Very few people knew about the fight that Johnny fought doing his duty in Vietnam, which was as challenging as the cancer.

He was buried in his family's plot with full honors that he had earned from his military service. His siblings mourned Johnny's death, and they would always remember him as their warrior hero.

Tom's recovery was slower than he had expected. The Army sent investigators to interview him about what happened on the patrol and how he missed boarding the Huey when it returned to the LZ. Tom didn't want to get his fellow soldiers in trouble, so he told the investigators that he had ventured into the jungle on his own and slipped on the wet foliage. He told him that when he fell, his head hit a tree and knocked him out.

Because he was unconscious, he didn't hear the Huey return, and that's how he ended up following the creek and the rest of the story. They seemed satisfied with his story and did not investigate further.

Tom's healing and recovery took several months, and then he was assigned to rehabilitation. He was able to transfer to an Army hospital that wasn't far from his hometown. His head wound healed nicely, and there were no long-term ill effects from the concussion. His crushed lung limited his breathing and endurance, so he had to find work that wasn't physically strenuous. Tom didn't like physical and strenuous work, so this fit Tom's personality perfectly. He didn't want to return to working in the factory, so he decided to follow in his grandfather's footsteps and work for the railroad.

He was hired as a yard clerk, where he would keep track of all the railcars and assign them to trains according to their destination. Because of Tom's treatment for his war injuries, he developed a dependency on the painkillers that were prescribed for him in the hospital.

The Veteran Rehab center worked with Tom to reduce, then eliminate, his dependency on drugs. Instead he switched to marijuana and alcohol to ease his pain. He was now popular in his hometown because of his heroics in Vietnam, so he didn't have a problem getting dates and spending a lot of time in bars. People enjoyed buying him drinks and sharing their pot with him. He was getting drunk and high on a nightly basis, and life for Tom was good.

One night, he was leaving one of the clubs and walking back to the railroad yard office, crossing the tracks to get to his truck. In his drunken and high state, he failed to see the freight train backing slowly. The train's engineer was moving cars, and there were no lights or a switchman on the back of the train. Tom saw he was on the same track as the train when it was only a few feet away from him. The train knocked him down, and he fell across the track. The train's wheel crushed him, killing Tom instantly.

Tom's funeral was as conducted the way he envisioned. There was a full military honor guard and ceremony. His funeral procession was held on the town's main street, with the sidewalks packed with people waving American flags, paying their last respects.

Tom never received the full recognition that he deserved from his country, but his hometown people knew of his heroics and that he was truly an American Hero.

He was buried in his hometown's cemetery in the section reserved for Veterans. His medals were on display at the funeral home and at the cemetery. Along with the American flag that had draped his casket, his mother was given his medals in a beautiful wooden case.

After Ben came home from his rehabilitation assignment, he found out that his girlfriend had married a college professor.

Although he was disappointed, he was quick to move on. He had bigger plans and wasn't going to let it get him down.

He had seen the devastation that war had on his fellow sailors and soldiers. He wanted to help them cope when they returned to the world, so he enrolled into college and studied psychology. He believed there was a method to help war Veterans open up and talk about their experiences, traumas, and fears from the war that would help them cope with society again.

Ben continued into graduate school and wrote his master's thesis on the unique issues that war veterans had to deal with and a possible alternative to their treatment. He received high marks for his work, and his professors recommended that he propose his treatment methods to the Veterans Administration (VA).

He arranged a meeting with the Psychiatric Department of the regional VA Hospital, and he was able to present his recommendations to the department chief and several other providers.

They politely listened to his recommendations, and then the department chief said to him, "Ben, your methods will not work. You're not experienced in treating war patients, and you need to follow the methods that we have already developed."

Interestingly, they offered Ben a job with the VA. Ben sat there in shock and said, "I appreciate your time, but I'm not interested in working at this VA hospital."

He chose instead to open his own therapy clinic, which took in patients who were able to pay or had insurance, as well as returning veterans, regardless of their ability to compensate him.

His clinic became a mecca for many veterans who had serious issues from serving in Vietnam and other conflicts. Ben's reputation grew, and other psychologists and psychiatrists joined his practice. They learned his methods and expanded the number of clients they were able to help.

Other clinics following Ben's treatment protocols were established in different parts of the country. The clinics were built in areas close to where Veteran soldiers had settled after coming back from Vietnam and other war zones.

The VA would not accept Ben's methods, and they continued to provide basic but ineffective treatment to combat veterans.

Finally, because of pressure from the American Legion and VFW, the Federal Government ordered a complete review on the VA medical service. It was determined to be ineffective, in fact failing the people it was supposed to be dedicated to serving. The VA, as with most government agencies, was slow with making changes to their practices.

Because of the continuing complaints for Veterans to senators and representatives, Congress threatened the VA's funding. Legislation was introduced to replace the VA's medical services with contracted providers. The changes and improvements have progressed slowly and are still being implemented today, over forty years since the end of the Vietnam War.

Ben was diagnosed with type 2 diabetes when he was fifty-two years old. Two years later, he developed a rare form of cancer that his doctors related directly to his exposure to Agent Orange and other chemicals used in Vietnam. Thankfully, he received the proper treatment in the early stages, and the cancer went into remission.

These five heroes had no interest in being anything except the people who they were. Their experiences and the trauma they suffered would never be shared totally with anyone. They knew that it was doubtful that anyone who hadn't experienced it could have understood their fight. When they returned to American soil and heard and saw the attitude of many Americans, they also understood that what they had been through would not be appreciated, so they buried their feelings and their stories deep within their minds, where they would return throughout their lives and torture them once more.

These five great Americans would never meet together again, but they would always remember each other, especially the man who saved them from an enemy that would have shown no mercy.

Five separate lives from different places, going in five different directions, but forever linked through their trauma and the miracle that saved them.

Epilogue

B EN CONTINUED TO treat Veterans and train counselors and other mental and emotional health providers. He addressed their issues, providing proper methods that were unique to Veterans yet would cross the thresholds of every war and conflict that our military has been involved with. His success rate and the providers who follow his methodology far exceeds the outcomes of the VA, and they are slowly and reluctantly beginning to adapt his methods.

These Vietnam Veterans were America's finest who served their country with honor and distinction at the highest level. They placed their lives on the line for their country in a misunderstood and misguided war. They were never given the recognition or the appreciation they deserved, but they did their duty for God and their Country. They did not leave the war in Vietnam but lived with it every day for the rest of their lives.

All would be heroes.

LIVE

listen|imagine|view|experience

AUDIO BOOK DOWNLOAD INCLUDED WITH THIS BOOK!

In your hands you hold a complete digital entertainment package. In addition to the paper version, you receive a free download of the audio version of this book. Simply use the code listed below when visiting our website. Once downloaded to your computer, you can listen to the book through your computer's speakers, burn it to an audio CD or save the file to your portable music device (such as Apple's popular iPod) and listen on the go!

How to get your free audio book digital download:

1. Visit www.tatepublishing.com and click on the e|LIVE logo on the home page.
2. Enter the following coupon code:
   0388-e3b4-8172-f10f-9ce5-8d86-b3c8-6f74
3. Download the audio book from your e|LIVE digital locker and begin enjoying your new digital entertainment package today!